William Black

Three Feathers

Vol. III

William Black

Three Feathers
Vol. III

ISBN/EAN: 9783337039837

Printed in Europe, USA, Canada, Australia, Japan

Cover: Foto ©Andreas Hilbeck / pixelio.de

More available books at **www.hansebooks.com**

A Novel.

BY WILLIAM BLACK,

AUTHOR OF

"A PRINCESS OF THULE," "A DAUGHTER OF HETH," ETC.

IN THREE VOLUMES.—Vol. III.

FOURTH EDITION.

LONDON:

SAMPSON LOW, MARSTON, LOW & SEARLE,

CROWN BUILDINGS, 188, FLEET STREET.

1875.

CONTENTS OF VOL. III.

THREE FEATHERS.

CHAPTER I.

MABYN DREAMS.

"Yes, mother," said Mabyn, bursting into the room, "here I am; and Jennifer's downstairs, with my box; and I am to stay with you here for another week or a fortnight; and Wenna's to go back at once, for the whole world is convulsed because of Mr. Trelyon's coming of age; and Mrs. Trelyon has sent and taken all our spare rooms; and father says Wenna must come back directly, for it's always 'Wenna, do this,' and 'Wenna, do that;' and if Wenna isn't there, of course the sky will tumble down on the earth——mother, what's the matter, and where's Wenna?"

Mabyn was suddenly brought up in the middle of her voluble speech by the strange expression on her mother's face.

"Oh, Mabyn, something dreadful has happened to our Wenna."

Mabyn turned deadly white.

"Is she ill?" she said, almost in a whisper.

"No, not ill; but a great trouble has fallen on her."

Then the mother, in a low voice, apparently fearful that any one should overhear, began to tell her younger daughter of all she had learnt within the past day or two—how young Trelyon had been bold enough to tell Wenna that he loved her; how Wenna had dallied with her conscience and been loth to part with him; how at length she had as good as revealed to him that she loved him in return ; and how she was now overwhelmed and crushed beneath a sense of her own faithlessness and the impossibility of making reparation to her betrothed.

"Only to think, Mabyn," said the mother, in accents of despair, "that all this distress should have come about in such a quiet and unexpected way! Who could have foreseen it? Why, of all people in the world, you would have thought our Wenna was the least likely to have any misery of this sort; and many a time, don't you remember, I used to say it was so wise of her getting engaged to a prudent and elderly man, who would save her from the plagues and trials that young girls often suffer at the hands of their lovers. I thought she was so comfortably settled. Everything promised her a quiet and gentle life. And now this sudden shock has come upon her, she seems to think she is not fit

to live, and she goes on in such a wild
way——"

"Where is she?" Mabyn said, abruptly.

"No, no, no," the mother said,
anxiously. "You must not speak a word
to her, Mabyn. You must not let her
know I have told you anything about it.
Leave her to herself for a while at least;
if you spoke to her, she would take it you
meant to accuse her; for she says you
warned her, and she would pay no heed.
Leave her to herself, Mabyn."

"Then where is Mr. Trelyon?" said
Mabyn, with some touch of indignation in
her voice. "What is he doing? Is he
leaving her to herself too?"

"I don't know what you mean, Mabyn,"
her mother said, timidly.

"Why doesn't he come forward like a
man, and marry her?" said Mabyn, boldly.
"Yes, that is what I would do, if I were a
man. She has sent him away? Yes, of

course. That is right and proper. And
Wenna will go on doing what is right and
proper, if you allow her, to the very end,
and the end will be a lifetime of misery,
that's all. No, my notion is that she
should do something that is not right and
is quite improper, if only it makes her
happy; and you'll see if I don't get her to
do it. Why, mother, haven't you had eyes
to see that these two have been in love for
years? Nobody in the world had ever the
least control over him but her; he would
do anything for Wenna; and she—why she
always came back singing after she had met
and spoken to him. And then you talk
about a prudent and sensible husband! I
don't want Wenna to marry a watchful,
mean, old, stocking-darning cripple, who
will creep about the house all day, and peer
into cupboards, and give her fourpence-half-
penny a week to live on. I want her to
marry a man, one that is strong enough to

protect her; and I tell you, mother—I've said it before and I say it again—she *shall not* marry Mr. Roscorla!"

"Mabyn!" said her mother, "you are getting madder than ever. Your dislike to Mr. Roscorla is most unreasonable. A cripple!—why——"

"Oh, mother!" Mabyn cried, with a bright light on her face, "only think of our Wenna being married to Mr. Trelyon, and how happy, and pleased, and pretty she would look as they went walking together! And then how proud he would be to have so nice a wife: and he would joke about her, and be very impertinent, but he would simply worship her all the same and do everything he could to please her. And he would take her away and show her all the beautiful places abroad; and he would have a yacht, too; and he would give her a fine house in London; and don't you think our Wenna would fascinate everybody with her

mouselike ways, and her nice, small steps?
And if they did have any trouble, wouldn't
she be better to have somebody with her,
not timid, and anxious, and pettifogging,
but somebody who wouldn't be cast down,
but make her as brave as himself?"

Miss Mabyn was a shrewd young
woman, and she saw that her mother's
quick, imaginative, sympathetic nature was
being captivated by this picture. She
determined to have her as an ally.

"And don't you see, mother, how it all
lies within her reach? Harry Trelyon is in
love with her—there was no need for him
to say so—I knew it long before he did.
And she—why, she has told him now that
she cares for him; and if I were he, I
know what I'd do in his place. What is
there in the way? Why, a—a sort of
understanding——"

"A promise, Mabyn," said the mother.

"Well, a promise," said the girl, desperately, and colouring somewhat. "But it was a promise given in ignorance—she didn't know—how could she know? Everybody knows that such promises are constantly broken. If you are in love with somebody else, what's the good of your keeping the promise? Now, mother, won't you argue with her? See here. If she keeps her promise, there's three people miserable. If she breaks it, there's only one—and I doubt whether he's got the capacity to be miserable. That's two to one, or three to one, is it? Now will you argue with her, mother?"

"Mabyn, Mabyn," the mother said, with a shake of the head, but evidently pleased with the voice of the tempter, "your fancy has run away with you. Why, Mr. Trelyon has never proposed to marry her."

"I know he wants to," said Mabyn, confidently.

"How can you know?"

"I'll ask him and prove it to you."

"Indeed," said the mother, sadly, "it is no thought of marriage that is in Wenna's head just now. The poor girl is full of remorse and apprehension. I think she would like to start at once for Jamaica, and fling herself at Mr. Roscorla's feet, and confess her fault. I am glad she has to go back to Eglosilyan; that may distract her mind in a measure; at present she is suffering more than she shows."

"Where is she?"

"In her own room, tired out and fast asleep. I looked in a few minutes ago."

Mabyn went upstairs, after having seen that Jennifer had properly bestowed her box. Wenna had just risen from the sofa, and was standing in the middle of the room. Her younger and taller sister went blithely forward to her, kissed her as usual, took no notice of the sudden flush of red that sprang into her face, and proceeded to state, in a business-like fashion, all the arrangements that had to be made.

"Have you been enjoying yourself, Wenna?" Mabyn said, with a fine air of indifference.

"Oh, yes," Wenna answered; adding hastily, "don't you think mother is greatly improved?"

"Wonderfully. I almost forgot she was an invalid. How lucky you are to be going back to see all the fine doings at the Hall; of course they will ask you up."

"They will do nothing of the kind," Wenna said, with some asperity, and with her face turned aside.

"Lord and Lady Amersham have already come to the Hall."

"Oh, indeed!"

"Yes; they said some time ago that there was a good chance of Mr. Trelyon marrying the daughter—the tall girl with yellow hair, you remember?"

"And the stooping shoulders? yes. I should think they would be glad to get her married to anybody. She's thirty."

"Oh, Wenna!"

"Mr. Trelyon told me so," said Wenna, sharply.

"And they are a little surprised," continued Mabyn, in the same indifferent way, but watching her sister all the while, "that Mr. Trelyon has remained absent until so near the time. But I suppose he means to take Miss Penaluna with him. She lives here, doesn't she? They used to say there was a chance of a marriage there, too."

"Mabyn, what do you mean?" Wenna said, suddenly and angrily. "What do I care about Mr. Trelyon's marriage? What is it you mean?"

But the firmness of her lips began to yield; there was an ominous trembling about them; and at the same moment her younger sister caught her to her bosom,

and hid her face there, and hushed her
wild sobbing. She would hear no confession. She knew enough. Nothing would
convince her that Wenna had done anything wrong; so there was no use speaking
about it.

"Wenna," she said, in a low voice,
"have you sent him any message?"

"Oh, no, no," the girl said, trembling.
"I fear even to think of him; and when
you mentioned his name, Mabyn, it seemed
to choke me. And now I have to go back
to Eglosilyan; and oh! if you only knew
how I dread that, Mabyn!"

Mabyn's conscience was struck. She it
was who had done this thing. She had
persuaded her father that her mother
needed another week or fortnight at Penzance; she had frightened him by telling him
what bother he would suffer if Wenna were
not back at the inn during the festivities
at Trelyon Hall: and then she had offered

to go and take her sister's post. George Rosewarne was heartily glad to exchange the one daughter for the other. Mabyn was too independent. She thwarted him; sometimes she insisted on his bestirring himself. Wenna, on the other hand, went about the place like some invisible spirit of order, making everything comfortable for him, without noise or worry. He was easily led to issue the necessary orders; and so it was that Mabyn thought she was doing her sister a friendly turn by sending her back to Eglosilyan in order to join in congratulating Harry Trelyon on his entrance into man's estate. Now Mabyn found that she had only plunged her sister into deeper trouble.

What could be done to save her?

"Wenna," said Mabyn, rather timidly, "do you think he has left Penzance?"

Wenna turned to her with a sudden look of entreaty in her face.

"1 cannot bear to speak of him, Mabyn.
I have no right to—I hope you will not
ask me.   Just now I—I am going to write
a letter—to Jamaica.   I shall tell the whole
truth.   It is for him to say what must
happen now.   I have done him a great
injury.   I did not intend it; I had no
thought of it; but my own folly and
thoughtlessness brought it about, and I
have to bear the penalty.   I don't think he
need be anxious about punishing me."

She turned away with a tired look on
her face, and began to get out her writing
materials.   Mabyn watched her for a moment or two in silence; then she left and
went to her own room, saying to herself,
"Punishment? whoever talks of punishment will have to address himself to me."

When she got to her own room, she
wrote these words on a piece of paper—in
her firm, bold, free hand—"*A friend would
like to see you for a minute in front of the*

Post Office in the middle of the town."
She put that in an envelope, and addressed
the envelope to Harry Trelyon, Esq. Still
keeping her bonnet on, she went downstairs, and had a little general conversation
with her mother, in the course of which she
quite casually asked the name of the hotel
at which Mr. Trelyon had been staying.
Then, just as if she were going out to the
parade to have a look at the sea, she carelessly left the house.

The dusk of the evening was growing to
dark. A white mist lay over the sea. The
solitary lamps were being lit along the
parade—each golden star shining sharply
in the pale purple twilight; but a more
confused glow of orange showed where the
little town was busy in its narrow thoroughfares. She got hold of a small boy, gave
him the letter, sixpence, and his instructions. He was to ask if the gentleman
were in the hotel. If not, had he left

Penzance, or would he return that night? In any case the boy was not to leave the letter unless Mr. Trelyon were there.

The small boy returned in a couple of minutes. The gentleman was there, and had taken the letter. So Mabyn at once set out for the centre of the town, and soon found herself in among a mass of huddled houses, bright shops, and thoroughfares pretty well filled with strolling sailors, women getting home from market, and townspeople come out to gossip. She had accurately judged that she would be less observed in this busy little place than out on the parade; and as it was the first appointment she had ever made to meet a young gentleman alone, she was just a little nervous.

. Trelyon was there. He had recognised the handwriting in a moment. He had no time to ridicule or even to think of Mabyn's schoolgirl affectation of secrecy; he had at once rushed off to the place of appointment, and that by a short cut of which she had no knowledge.

" Mabyn, what's the matter ? Is Wenna ill ? " he said—forgetting in his anxiety even to shake hands with her.

" Oh no, she isn't," said Mabyn, rather coldly and defiantly. If he was in love with her sister, it was for him to make advances.

" Oh no, she's pretty well, thank you," continued Mabyn, indifferently. " But she never could stand much worry. I wanted to see you about that. She is going back to Eglosilyan to-morrow; and you must promise not to have her asked up to the Hall while these grand doings are going on —you must not try to see her and persuade her—if you could keep out of her way altogether——"

" You know all about it, then, Mabyn ? " he said, suddenly; and even in the dusky

light of the street, she could see the rapid
look of gladness that filled his face. "And
you are not going to be vexed, eh? You'll
remain friends with me, Mabyn—you will
tell me how she is from time to time.
Don't you see I must go away—and, by
Jove, Mabyn, I've got such a lot to tell you!"

She looked round.

"I can't talk to you here. Won't you
walk back by the other road behind the
town?" he said.

Yes, she would go willingly with him
now. The anxiety of his face, the almost
wild way in which he seemed to beg for her
help and friendship, the mere impatience of
his manner pleased and satisfied her. This
was as it should be. Here was no sweetheart by line and rule, demonstrating his
affection by argument, acting at all times
with a studied propriety; but a real, true
lover, full of passionate hope and as passionate fear, ready to do anything, and yet

not knowing what to do. Above all he was "brave and handsome, like a prince!" and therefore a fit lover for her gentle sister.

"Oh, Mr. Trelyon," she said, with a great burst of confidence, "I did so fear that you might be indifferent!"

"Indifferent!" said he, with some bitterness. "Perhaps that is the best thing that could happen; only it isn't very likely to happen. Did you ever see anybody placed as I am placed, Mabyn? Nothing but stumbling-blocks every way I look. Our family have always been hot-headed and hot-tempered; if I told my grandmother at this minute how I am situated, I believe she would say, 'Why don't you go like a man, and run off with the girl?'——"

"Yes!" said Mabyn, quite delighted.

"But suppose you've bothered and worried the girl until you feel ashamed of yourself, and she begs of you to leave her, aren't you bound in fair manliness to go?"

"I don't know," said Mabyn, doubt-fully.

"Well, I do. It would be very mean to pester her. I'm off as soon as these people leave the Hall. But then there are other things. There is your sister engaged to this fellow out in Jamaica ——"

"Isn't he a horrid wretch?" said Mabyn, between her teeth.

"Oh, I quite agree with you. If I could have it out with him now—— but after all, what harm has the man done? Is it any wonder he wanted to get Wenna for a wife?"

"Oh, but he cheated her," said Mabyn, warmly. "He persuaded her, and reasoned with her, and argued her into marrying him. And what business had he to tell her that love between young people is all bitterness and trial; and that a girl is only safe when she marries a prudent and elderly man who will look after her? Why, it is to look after him that he wants her. Wenna is going to him as a housekeeper and a nurse. Only—only, Mr. Trelyon, *she hasn't gone to him just yet!*"

"Oh, I don't think he did anything unfair," the young man said, gloomily. "It doesn't matter anyhow. What I was going to say is that my grandmother's notion of what one of our family ought to do in such a case can't be carried out: whatever you may think of a man, you can't go and try to rob him of his sweetheart behind his back. Even supposing she was willing to break with him, which she is not, you've at least got to wait to give the fellow a chance."

"There I quite disagree with you, Mr. Trelyon," Mabyn said, warmly. "Wait to give him a chance to make our Wenna miserable? Is she to be made the prize of a sort of fight? If I were a man, I'd pay less attention to my own scruples and try

what I could do for her. . . . Oh, Mr. Trelyon—I—I beg your pardon."

Mabyn suddenly stopped on the road,
overwhelmed with confusion. She had been
so warmly thinking of her sister's welfare
that she had been hurried into something
worse than an indiscretion.

" What, then, Mabyn ? " said he, pro-
foundly surprised.

" I beg your pardon. I have been so
thoughtless. I had no right to assume that
you wished—that you wished for the—for
the opportunity——"

" Of marrying Wenna ? " said he, with a
great stare. " But what else have we been
speaking about ? Or rather, I suppose we
did assume it. Well, the more I think of it,
Mabyn, the more I am maddened by all
these obstacles, and by the notion of all
the things that may happen. That's the
bad part of my going away. How can I
tell what may happen ? He might come

back, and insist on her marrying him right
off."

"Mr. Trelyon," said Mabyn, speaking
very clearly, "there's one thing you may be
sure of. If you let me know where you are,
nothing will happen to Wenna that you
don't hear of."

He took her hand, and pressed it in
mute thankfulness. He was not insensible
to the value of having so warm an advocate,
so faithful an ally, always at Wenna's side.

"How long do letters take in going to
Jamaica?" Mabyn asked.

"I don't know."

"I could fetch him back for you
directly," said she, "if you would like
that."

"How?"

"By writing and telling him that you
and Wenna were going to get married.
Wouldn't that fetch him back pretty
quickly?"

"I doubt it. He wouldn't believe it of Wenna. Then he is a sensible sort of fellow, and would say to himself that, if the news was true, he would have his journey for nothing. Besides, Barnes says that things are looking well with him in Jamaica—better than anybody expected. He might not be anxious to leave."

They had now got back to the parade, and Mabyn stopped.

"I must leave you now, Mr. Trelyon. Mind not to go near Wenna when you get to Eglosilyan——"

"She shan't even see me. I shall be there only a couple of days or so; then I am going to London. I am going to have a try at the Civil Service examinations—for first commissions, you know. I shall only come back to Eglosilyan for a day now and again at long intervals. You have promised to write to me, Mabyn—well, I'll send you my address."

She looked at him keenly as she offered him her hand.

"I wouldn't be down-hearted if I were you," she said. "Very odd things sometimes happen."

"Oh, I shan't be very down-hearted," said he, "so long as I hear that she is all right, and not vexing herself about anything."

"Good-bye, Mr. Trelyon. I am sorry I can't take any message for you."

"To her? No, that is impossible. Good bye, Mabyn; I think you are the best friend I have in the world."

"We'll see about that," she said, as she walked rapidly off.

Her mother had been sufficiently astonished by her long absence; she was now equally surprised by the excitement and pleasure visible in her face.

"Oh, mammy, do you know whom I've seen? Mr. Trelyon!"

" Mabyn ! "

" Yes. We've walked right round Penzance—all by ourselves. And it's all settled, mother."

" What is all settled ? "

" The understanding between him and me. An offensive and defensive alliance. Let tyrants beware ! "

She took off her bonnet, and came and sat down on the floor by the side of the sofa.

" Oh, mammy, I see such beautiful things in the future—you wouldn't believe it if I told you all I see ! Everybody else seems determined to forecast such gloomy events—there's Wenna crying and writing letters of contrition, and expecting all sorts of anger and scolding ; there's Mr. Trelyon, haunted by the notion that Mr. Roscorla will suddenly come home and marry Wenna right off; and as for him out there in Jamaica, I expect he'll be in a nice state when he hears of all this. But far on ahead of all that I see such a beautiful picture——"

"It is a dream of yours, Mabyn," her mother said; but there was an imaginative light in her fine eyes, too.

"No, it is not a dream, mother; for there are so many people all wishing now that it should come about, in spite of these gloomy fancies. What is there to prevent it, when we are all agreed? Mr. Trelyon and I heading the list with our important alliance; and you mother, would be so proud to see Wenna happy; and Mrs. Trelyon pets her as if she were a daughter already, and everybody — every man, woman, and child in Eglosilyan would rather see that come about than get a guinea apiece. Oh, mother, if you could see the picture that I see just now——"

"It is a pretty picture, Mabyn," her mother said, shaking her head. "But when you think of everybody being agreed, you forget one, and that is Wenna herself. Whatever she thinks fit and right to do, that she is certain to do; and all your alliances and friendly wishes won't alter her decision, even if it should break her heart. And, indeed, I hope the poor child won't sink under the terrible strain that is on her: what do you think of her looks, Mabyn?"

"They want mending; yes, they want mending," Mabyn admitted, apparently with some compunction; but then she added, boldly, "and you know as well as I do, mother, that there is but the one way of mending them!"

CHAPTER II.

FERN IN DIE WELT.

IF this story were not tied by its title to the Duchy of Cornwall, it might be interesting enough to follow Mr. Roscorla into the new world that had opened all around him, and say something of the sudden shock his old habits had thus received, and of the quite altered views of his own life he had been led to form. As matters stand, we can only pay him a flying visit.

He is seated in a verandah, fronting a garden, in which pomegranates and oranges form the principal fruit. Down below him some blacks are bringing provisions up to Yacca Farm, along the cactus avenue leading to the gate. Far away on his right, the last rays of the sun are shining on the summit of Blue Mountain Peak; and along the horizon the reflected glow of the sky shines on the calm sea. It is a fine, still evening; his cigar smells sweet in the air; it is a time for indolent dreaming and for memories of home.

But Mr. Roscorla is not so much enraptured by thoughts of home as he might be.

"Why," he is saying to himself, "my life in Basset Cottage was no life at all, but only a waiting for death. Day after day passed in that monotonous fashion; what had one to look forward to but old age, sickness, and then the quiet of a coffin? It was nothing but an hourly procession to the grave, varied by rabbit-shooting. This bold breaking away from the narrow life of such a place has given me a new lease of existence. Now I can look back with surprise

on the dulness of that Cornish village, and
on the regularity of habits which I did not
know were habits. For is not that always
the case? You don't know that you are
forming a habit; you take each act to be an
individual act, which you may perform or
not at will; but all the same the succession
of them is getting you into its power,
custom gets a grip of your ways of thinking
as well as your ways of living; the habit is
formed, and it does not cease its hold until
it conducts you to the grave. Try Jamaica
for a cure. Fling a sleeping man into the
sea, and watch if he does not wake. Why,
when I look back to the slow, methodical,
commonplace life I led at Eglosilyan, can I
wonder that I˙ was sometimes afraid of
Wenna Rosewarne regarding me as a somewhat staid and venerable person, on whose
infirmities she ought to take pity? "

He rose and began to walk up and down
the verandah, putting his foot down firmly.

His loose linen suit was smart enough; his complexion had been improved by the sun. The consciousness that his business affairs were promising well did not lessen his sense of self-importance.

"Wenna must be prepared to move about a bit when I go back," he was saying to himself. "She must give up that daily attendance on cottagers' children. If all turns out well, I don't see why we should not live in London; for who will know there who her father was? That consideration was of no consequence so long as I looked forward to living the rest of my life in Basset Cottage; now there are other things to be thought of when there is a chance of my going among my old friends again."

By this time, it must be observed, Mr. Roscorla had abandoned his hasty intention of returning to England to upbraid Wenna with having received a ring from Harry

Trelyon. After all, he reasoned with himself, the mere fact that she should talk thus simply and frankly about young Trelyon showed that, so far as she was concerned, her loyalty to her absent lover was unbroken. As for the young gentleman himself, he was, Mr. Roscorla knew, fond of joking. He had doubtless thought it a fine thing to make a fool of two or three women by imposing on them this cock-and-bull story of finding a ring by dredging. He was a little angry that Wenna should have been deceived ; but then, he reflected, these gipsy-rings are so much like one another that the young man had probably got a pretty fair duplicate. For the rest, he did not want to quarrel with Harry Trelyon at present.

But as he was walking up and down this verandah, looking a much younger and brisker man than the Mr. Roscorla who had left Eglosilyan, a servant came through the house and brought him a couple of letters. He saw they were respectively from Mr. Barnes and from Wenna; and, curiously enough, he opened the reverend gentleman's first—perhaps as schoolboys like to leave the best bit of a tart to the last.

He read the letter over carefully; he sat down and read it again; then he put it before him on the table. He was evidently puzzled by it.

"What does this man mean by writing these letters to me?"—so Mr. Roscorla, who was a cautious and reflective person, communed with himself. "He is no particular friend of mine. He must be driving at something. Now he says that I am to be of good cheer. I must not think anything of what he formerly wrote. Mr. Trelyon is leaving Eglosilyan for good, and his mother will at last have some peace of mind. What a pity it is that this sensitive creature should be at the mercy of the rude passions of this son of hers—that she should have no protector—that she should be allowed to mope herself to death in a melancholy seclusion."

An odd fancy occurred to Mr. Roscorla at this moment, and he smiled.

"I think I have got a clue to Mr. Barnes's disinterested anxiety about my affairs. The widower would like to protect the solitary and unfriended widow; but the young man is in the way. The young man would be very much in the way if he married Wenna Rosewarne; the widower's fears drive him into suspicion, then into certainty; nothing will do but that I should return to England at once, and spoil this little arrangement. But as soon as Harry Trelyon declares his intention of leaving Eglosilyan for good, then my affairs may go anyhow. Mr. Barnes finds the coast clear; I am bidden to stay where I am. Well, that is what I mean to do; but now

I fancy I understand Mr. Barnes's generous friendship for me and his affectionate correspondence."

He turned to Wenna's letter with much compunction. He owed her some atonement for having listened to the disingenuous reports of this scheming clergyman. How could he have so far forgotten the firm, uncompromising rectitude of the girl's character, her sensitive notions of honour, the promises she had given?

He read the letter, and as he read his eyes seemed to grow hot with rage. He paid no heed to the passionate contrition of the trembling lines; to the obvious pain that she had endured in telling the story, without concealment, against herself; to the utter and abject wretchedness with which she awaited his decision. It was thus that she had kept faith with him the moment his back was turned. Such were the safeguards afforded by a woman's sense of honour. What a fool he had been, to imagine that any woman could remain true to her promise, so soon as some other object of flirtation and incipient love-making came in her way!

He looked at the letter again: he could scarcely believe it to be in her handwriting. This the quiet, reasonable, gentle, and timid Wenna Rosewarne, whose virtues were almost a trifle too severe? The despair and remorse of the letter did not touch him—he was too angry and indignant over the insult to himself—but it astonished him. The passionate emotion of those closely-written pages he could scarcely connect with the shy, frank, kindly little girl he remembered; it was a cry of agony from a tortured woman, and he knew at least that for her the old, quiet time was over.

He knew not what to do. All this that had happened was new to him; it was old and gone by in England, and who could tell what further complications might have arisen? But his anger required some vent; he went indoors, called for a lamp, and sat down and wrote, with a hard and resolute look on his face :—

"I have received your letter. I am not surprised. You are a woman; and I ought to have known that a woman's promise is of value so long as you are by her side to see that she keeps it. You ask what reparation you can make; I ask if there is any that you can suggest. No; you have done what cannot be undone. Do you think a man would marry a woman who is in love with, or has been in love with another man, even if he could overlook her breach of faith and the shameless thoughtlessness of her conduct? My course is clear, at all events. I give you back the promise that you did not know how to keep; and now you can go and ask the young man who has been making a holiday toy of you whether he will be pleased to marry you.

"RICHARD ROSCORLA."

He sealed and addressed this letter, still with the firm, hard look about his face; then he summoned a servant—a tall, red-haired Irishman. He did not hesitate for a moment.

"Look here, Sullivan, the English mails go out to-morrow morning—you must ride down to the Post Office, as hard as you can go; and if you're a few minutes late, see Mr. Keith, and give him my compliments, and ask him if he can possibly take this letter if the mails are not made up. It is of great importance. Quick now!"

He watched the man go clattering down the cactus avenue until he was out of sight. Then he turned, put the letters in his pocket, went indoors, and again struck a small gong that did duty for a bell. He wanted his horse brought round at once. He was going over to Pleasant Farm; probably he would not return that night. He lit another cigar and paced up and down the gravel in front of the house until the horse was brought round.

When he reached Pleasant Farm, the stars were shining overhead, and the odours of the night-flowers came floating out of the forest; but inside the house there were brilliant lights and the voices of men talking. A bachelor supper-party was going forward. Mr. Roscorla entered, and presently was seated at the hospitable board.

They had never seen him so gay; and they had certainly never seen him so generously inclined, for Mr. Roscorla was economical in his habits. He would have them all to dinner the next evening, and promised them such champagne as had never been sent to Kingston before. He passed round his best cigars; he hinted something about unlimited loo; he drank pretty freely; and was altogether in a jovial humour.

"England?" he said, when some one mentioned the mother country. "Of one thing I am pretty certain—England will never see me again. No—a man lives here; in England he waits for his death. What life I have got before me I shall live in Jamaica—that is my view of the question."

"Then she is coming out to you?" said his host, with a grin.

Roscorla's face flushed with anger.

"There is no she in the matter," he said, abruptly, almost fiercely. "I thank God I am not tied to any woman."

"Oh, I beg your pardon," said his host, good-naturedly, who did not care to recall the occasions on which Mr. Roscorla had been rather pleased to admit that certain tender ties bound him to his native land.

"No, there is not!" he said. "What fool would have his comfort and peace of mind depend on the caprice of a woman? I like your plan better, Rogers: when they're dependent on you, you can do as you like; but when they've got to be treated as equals, they're the devil. No, my boys, you don't find me going in for the angel in the house—she's too exacting. Is it to be unlimited?"

Now to play unlimited loo in a reckless fashion is about the easiest way of getting rid of money that the ingenuity of man has devised. The other players were much better qualified to run such risks than Mr. Roscorla; but none played half so wildly as he. I.O.U's went freely about. At one point in the evening the floating paper bearing the signature of Mr. Roscorla represented a sum of about 300*l*.; and yet his losses did not weigh heavily on him. At length every one got tired, and it was resolved to stop short at a certain hour. But from this point the luck changed; nothing could stand against his cards; one by one his I.O.U's were recalled; and when they all rose from the table, he had won about 48*l.* He was not elated.

He went to his room, and sat down in an easy-chair; and then it seemed to him that he saw Eglosilyan once more, and the far coasts of Cornwall, and the broad uplands lying under a blue English sky. That was his home, and he had cut himself away from it, and from the little glimmer of romance that had recently brightened it for him. Every bit of the place, too, was associated somehow with Wenna Rosewarne. He could see the seat, fronting the Atlantic, on which she used to sit and sew on the fine summer forenoons. He could see the rough road, leading over the downs, on which he met her one wintry morning, she wrapped up and driving her father's dog-cart, while the red sun in the sky seemed to brighten the pink colour the cold wind had brought into her cheeks. He thought of her walking sedately up to church; of her wild scramblings among the rocks with Mabyn; of her enjoyment of a fierce wind when it came laden with the spray of the great rollers breaking on the cliff outside. What was the song she used to sing to herself as she went along the quiet woodland ways?—

Your Polly has never been false, she declares,
Since last time we parted at Wapping Old Stairs.

He could not let her go. All the anger of wounded vanity had left his heart; he thought now only of the chance he was throwing away. Where else could he hope to find for himself so pleasant a companion and friend, who would cheer up his dull daily life with her warm sympathies, her quick humour, her winning womanly ways?

He thought of that letter he had sent

away, and cursed his own folly. So long as she was bound by her promise, he knew he could marry her when he pleased; but now he had voluntarily released her. In a couple of weeks she would hold her manumission in her hands; the past would no longer have any power over her; if ever they met, they would meet as mere acquaintances. Every moment the prize slipping out of his grasp seemed to grow more valuable; his vexation with himself grew intolerable; he suddenly resolved that he would make a wild effort to get back that fatal letter.

He had sat communing with himself for over an hour; all the household was fast asleep. He would not wake any one, for fear of being compelled to give explanations; so he noiselessly crept along the dark passages until he got to the door, which he carefully opened and let himself out. The night was wonderfully clear; the

constellations throbbing and glittering overhead; the trees were black against the pale
sky.

He made his way round to the stables,
and had some sort of notion that he would
try to get at his horse, until it occurred
to him that some suddenly awakened servant or master would probably send a bullet
whizzing at him. So he abandoned that
enterprise, and set off to walk, as quickly as
he could, down the slopes of the mountain,
with the stars still shining over his head,
the air sweet with powerful scents, the
leaves of the bushes hanging silently in the
semi-darkness.

How long he walked he did not know;
he was not aware that, when he reached the
sleeping town, a pale grey was lightening
the eastern skies. He went to the house of
the postmaster and hurriedly aroused him.
Mr. Keith began to think that the ordinarily
sedate Mr. Roscorla had gone mad.

"But I must have the letter," he said. "Come now, Keith, you can give it me back if you like. Of course, I know it is very wrong; but you'll do it to oblige a friend——"

"My dear sir," said the postmaster, who could not get time for explanation, "the mails were made up last night——"

"Yes, yes; but you can open the English bag."

"They were sent on board last night."

"Then the packet is still in the harbour; you might come down with me——"

"She sails at daybreak——"

"It is not daybreak yet," said Mr. Roscorla, looking up.

Then he saw how the grey dawn had come over the skies, banishing the stars, and he became aware of the wan light shining around him. With the new day his life was altered; he would no more be as he had been; the chief aim and purpose of his existence had been changed.

Walking heedlessly back, he came to a point from which he had a distant view of the harbour and the sea beyond. Far away out on the dull grey plain was a steamer slowly making her way towards the east. Was that the packet bound for England, carrying to Wenna Rosewarne the message that she was free?

CHAPTER III.

"BLUE IS THE SWEETEST."

THE following correspondence may now, without any great breach of confidence, be published :—

                 "*Eglosilyan, Monday morning.*

"DEAR MR. TRELYON,

         "Do you know what Mr. Roscorla says in the letter Wenna has just received? Why, that you could not get up that ring by dredging, but that you must have bought the ring at Plymouth. Just think of the wicked old wretch fancying such things; as if you would give a ring *of emeralds to any one!* Tell me that this is a story, that I may bid Wenna contradict him at once. I have got no patience with a man who is given over to such mean suspicions.

"Yours faithfully,

"MABYN ROSEWARNE."

"*London, Tuesday night.*

"DEAR MABYN,

"I am sorry to say Mr. Roscorla is right. It was a foolish trick—I did not think it would be successful, for my hitting the size of her finger was rather a stroke of luck; but I thought it would amuse her if she did find it out after an hour or two. I was afraid to tell her afterwards, for she would think it impertinent. What's to be done? Is she angry about it?

"Yours sincerely,

"HARRY TRELYON."

"*Eglosilyan.*

"DEAR MR. TRELYON,

"How could you do such a thing! Why, to give Wenna, of all people in the

world, an emerald ring, just after I had got
Mr. Roscorla to give her one, for bad luck
to himself! Why, how could you do it! I
don't know what to say about it—unless
you demand it back, *and send her one with
sapphires in it at once.*

" Yours,

" M. R.

" P.S.—*As quick as ever you can.*"

" *London, Friday morning.*

" DEAR MABYN,

" Why, you know she wouldn't
take a sapphire ring or any other from me.

" Yours faithfully,

" H. TRELYON."

" MY DEAR MR. TRELYON,

" Pray don't lose any time in writing; but send me at once a sapphire ring
for Wenna. You have hit the size once,
and you can do it again; but in any case, I
have marked the size on this bit of thread,

and the jeweller will understand. And
please, dear Mr. Trelyon, don't get a very
expensive one, but a plain, good one, just
like what a poor person like me would buy
for a present, if I wanted to. And post
it at once, please—*this is very important.*

"Yours most sincerely,

"MABYN ROSEWARNE."

In consequence of this correspondence,
Mabyn, one morning, proceeded to seek out
her sister, whom she found busy with the
accounts of the Sewing Club, which was
now in a flourishing condition. Mabyn
seemed a little shy.

"Oh, Wenna," she said, "I have something to tell you. You know I wrote to ask
Mr. Trelyon about the ring. Well, he's
very, very sorry—oh, you don't know how
sorry he is, Wenna!—but it's quite true.
He thought he would please you by getting
the ring, and that you would make a joke of

it when you found it out; and then he was
afraid to speak of it afterwards——"

Wenna had quietly slipped the ring off
her finger. She betrayed no emotion at the
mention of Mr. Trelyon's name. Her face
was a trifle red, that was all.

"It was a stupid thing to do," she said,
"but I suppose he meant no harm. Will
you send him back the ring?"

"Yes," she said, eagerly. "Give me
the ring, Wenna."

She carefully wrapped it up in a piece of
paper, and put it in her pocket. Any one
who knew her would have seen by her face
that she meant to give that ring short shrift.
Then she said timidly—

"You are not very angry, Wenna?"

"No. I am sorry I should have vexed
Mr. Roscorla by my carelessness."

"Wenna," the younger sister continued,
even more timidly, "do you know what I've
heard about rings—that when you've worn

one for some time on a finger, you ought never to leave it off altogether; I think it affects the circulation—or something of that kind. Now if Mr. Trelyon were to send you another ring, just to—to keep the place of that one until Mr. Roscorla came back——"

"Mabyn you must be mad to think of such a thing," said her sister, looking down.

"Oh, yes," Mabyn said, meekly, "I thought you wouldn't like the notion of Mr. Trelyon giving you a ring. And so, dear Wenna, I've—I've got a ring for you—you won't mind taking it from me; and if you do wear it on the engaged finger, why, that doesn't matter, don't you see——"

She produced the ring of dark blue stones, and herself put it on Wenna's finger.

"Oh, Mabyn," Wenna said, "how could you be so extravagant! And just after you gave me that ten shillings for the Leans."

"You be quiet," said Mabyn, briskly, going off with a light look on her face.

And yet there was some determination about her mouth. She hastily put on her hat, and went out. She took the path by the hillside over the little harbour; and eventually she reached the face of Black Cliff, at the foot of which a grey-green sea was dashing in white masses of foam; there was no living thing around her but the choughs and daws, and the white sea-gulls sailing overhead.

She took out a large sheet of brown paper and placed it on the ground. Then she sought out a bit of rock, weighing about two pounds. Then she took out the little parcel which contained the emerald ring, tied it up carefully along with the stone in the sheet of brown paper; finally, she rose up to her full height and heaved the whole into the sea. A splash down there, and that was all.

She clapped her hands with joy.

" And now my precious emerald ring, that's the last of you, I imagine! And there isn't much chance of a fish bringing you back, to make mischief with your ugly green stones! "

Then she went home, and wrote this note :—

" Eglosilyan, Monday.

" DEAR MR. TRELYON,

" I have just thrown the emerald ring you gave Wenna into the sea, and she wears the other one now <i>on her engaged finger</i>, but she thinks I bought it. Did you ever hear of an old-fashioned rhyme that is this ?—

O, green is forsaken,
And yellow's forsworn,
And blue is the sweetest
Colour that's worn !

You can't tell what mischief that emerald ring might not have done. But the sapphires that Wenna is wearing now are perfectly beautiful; and Wenna is not so heartbroken that she isn't very proud of them. I never saw such a beautiful ring.

" Yours sincerely,

" MABYN ROSEWARNE.

" P.S.—Are you never coming back to Eglosilyan any more ? "

So the days went by, and Mabyn waited, with a secret hope, to see what answer Mr. Roscorla would send to that letter of confession and contrition Wenna had written to him at Penzance. The letter had been written as an act of duty, and posted too ; but there was no mail going out for ten days thereafter, so that a considerable time had to elapse before the answer came.

During that time Wenna went about her ordinary duties, just as if there was no hidden fire of pain consuming her heart; there was no word spoken by her or to her

of all that had recently occurred; her mother
and sister were glad to see her so con-
,tinuously busy.   At first she shrank from
going up to Trelyon Hall, and would rather
have corresponded with Mrs. Trelyon about
their joint work of charity, but she conquered the feeling, and went and saw the
gentle lady, who perceived nothing altered
or strange in her demeanour.   At last the
letter from Jamaica came; and Mabyn,
having sent it up to her sister's room,
waited for a few minutes, and then followed it.   She was a little afraid, despite
her belief in the virtues of the sapphire
ring.

When she entered the room, she uttered
a slight cry of alarm and ran forward to her
sister.   Wenna was seated on a chair by the
side of the bed, but she had thrown her
arms out on the bed, her head was between
them, and she was sobbing as if her heart
would break.

"Wenna, what is the matter? what has he said to you?"

Mabyn's eyes were all afire now. Wenna would not answer. She would not even raise her head.

"Wenna, I want to see that letter."

"Oh, no, no," the girl moaned. "I deserve it; he says what is true; I want you to leave me alone, Mabyn—you—you can't do anything to help this——"

But Mabyn had by this time perceived that her sister held in her hand, crumpled up, the letter which was the cause of this wild outburst of grief. She went forward and firmly took it out of the yielding fingers; then she turned to the light and read it.

"Oh, if I were a man!" she said; and then the very passion of her indignation, finding no other vent, filled her eyes with proud and angry tears. She forgot to rejoice that her sister was now free. She only saw the cruel insult of those lines, and the fashion in which it had struck down its victim.

"Wenna," she said, hotly, "you ought to have more spirit! You don't mean to say you care for the opinion of a man who would write to any girl like that! You ought to be precious glad that he has shown himself in his true colours. Why, he never cared a bit for you—never!—or he would never turn at a moment's notice and insult you——"

"I have deserved it all; it is every word of it true; he could not have written otherwise "—that was all that Wenna would say between her sobs.

"Well," retorted Mabyn, "after all I am glad he was angry. I did not think he had so much spirit. And if this is his opinion of you, I don't think it is worth heeding, only I hope he'll keep to it. Yes, I do! I hope he'll continue to think you everything that is wicked, and remain out in Jamaica. Wenna, you must not lie and cry like that. Come, get up, and look at the strawberries that Mr. Trewhella has sent you."

"Please, Mabyn, leave me alone, there's a good girl."

"I shall be up again in a few minutes, then; I want you to drive me over to St. Gwennis. Wenna, I *must* go over to St. Gwennis before lunch; and father won't let me have anybody to drive; do you hear, Wenna?"

Then she went out and down into the kitchen, where she bothered Jennifer for a few minutes until she had got an iron heated at the fire. With this implement she carefully smoothed out the crumpled letter, and then she as carefully folded it, took it upstairs, and put it safely away in her own desk. She had just time to write a few lines :—

" Dear Mr. Trelyon,

"Do you know what news I have
got to tell you? Can you guess? The
engagement between Mr. Roscorla and
Wenna *is broken off;* and I have got in
my possession the letter in which he sets
her free. If you knew how glad I am!—
I should like to cry 'Hurrah! hurrah!' all
through the streets of Eglosilyan, and I
think every one else would do the same
if only they knew. Of course, she is very
much grieved, for he has been most in-
sulting. I cannot tell you the things he
has said; you would kill him if you heard
them. But she will come round very soon,
I know; and then she will have her freedom again, and no more emerald rings, and
letters all filled with arguments. Would
you like to see her, Mr. Trelyon? But
don't come yet—not for a long time—
she would only get angry and obstinate.
I'll tell you when to come; and in the

meantime, you know, she is still wearing
your ring, so that you need not be afraid.
How glad I shall be to see you again!

"Yours most faithfully,

"MABYN ROSEWARNE."

She went downstairs quickly, and put
this letter in the letter-box. There was an
air of triumph on her face. She had worked
for this result—aided by the mysterious
powers of fate, whom she had conjured to
serve her—and now the welcome end of her
labours had arrived. She bade the ostler
get out the dog-cart, as if she were the
Queen of Sheba going to visit Solomon.
She went marching up to her sister's room,
announcing her approach with a more than
ordinarily accurate rendering of "Oh, the
men of merry, merry England!" so that a
stranger might have fancied that he heard
the very voice of Harry Trelyon, with all
its unmelodious vigour, ringing along the
passage.

CHAPTER IV.

THE EXILE'S RETURN.

PERHAPS you have been away in distant parts of the earth, each day crowded with new experiences and slowly obscuring the clear pictures of England with which you left; perhaps you have only been hidden away in London, amid its ceaseless noise, its strange faces, its monotonous recurrence of duties; let us say, in any case, that you are returning home for a space to the quiet of northern Cornwall.

You look out of the high window of a Plymouth hotel early in the morning; there is promise of a beautiful autumn day. A ring of pink mist lies around the horizon;

overhead the sky is clear and blue; the
white sickle of the moon still lingers visible.
The new warmth of the day begins to melt
the hoar-frost in the meadows, and you
know that out beyond the town the sun is
shining brilliantly on the wet grass, with
the brown cattle gleaming red in the light.

You leave the great world behind, with
all its bustle, crowds, and express engines,
when you get into the quiet little train
that takes you leisurely up to Launceston,
through woods, by the sides of rivers, over
great valleys. There is a sense of repose
about this railway journey. The train
stops at any number of small stations—
apparently to let the guard have a chat
with the station-master—and then jogs on
in a quiet, contented fashion. And on such
an autumn day as this, that is a beautiful,
still, rich-coloured, and English-looking
country through which it passes. Here is
a deep valley, all glittering with the dew

and the sunlight. Down in the hollow a farm-yard is half hidden behind the yellowing elms; a boy is driving a flock of white geese along the twisting road; the hedges are red with the withering briers. Up here, along the hillsides, the woods of scrub oak are glowing with every imaginable hue of gold, crimson, and bronze, except where a few dark firs appear, or where a tuft of broom, pure and bright in its green, stands out among the faded brackens. The gorse is profusely in bloom —it always is in Cornwall. Still further over there are sheep visible on the uplands; beyond these again the bleak brown moors rise into peaks of hills; overhead the silent blue, and all around the sweet, fresh country air.

With a sharp whistle the small train darts into an opening in the hills; here we are in the twilight of a great wood. The tall trees are becoming bare; the ground is red with the fallen leaves; through the branches the blue-winged jay flies, screaming harshly; you can smell the damp and resinous odours of the ferns. Out again we get into the sunlight; and lo! a rushing, brawling, narrow stream, its clear flood swaying this way and that by the big stones; a wall of rock overhead crowned by glowing furze; a herd of red cattle sent scampering through the bright-green grass. Now we get slowly into a small white station, and catch a glimpse of a tiny town over in the valley; again we go on by wood and valley, by rocks, and streams, and farms. It is a pleasant drive on such a morning.

In one of the carriages in this train Master Harry Trelyon and his grandmother were seated. How he had ever persuaded her to go with him to Cornwall by train was mysterious enough; for the old lady thoroughly hated all such modern devices.

It was her custom to go travelling all over the country with a big, old-fashioned phaeton and a pair of horses; and her chief amusement during these long excursions was driving up to any big house she took a fancy to, in order to see if there was a chance of its being let to her. The faithful old servant who attended her, and who was about as old as the coachman, had a great respect for his mistress; but sometimes he swore — inaudibly — when she ordered him to make the usual inquiry at the front-door of some noble lord's country residence, which he would as soon have thought of letting as of forfeiting his seat in the House of Peers or his hopes of heaven. But the carriage and horses were coming down all the same to Eglosilyan, to take her back again.

"Harry," she was saying at this moment, "the longer I look at you, the more positive I am that you are ill. I don't like

your colour; you are thin, and careworn,
and anxious. What is the matter with
you ? "

" Going to school again at twenty-one is
hard work, grandmother," he said. " Don't
you try it. But I don't think I'm particularly ill; few folks can keep a complexion
like yours, grandmother."

" Yes," said the old lady, rather pleased,
" many's the time they said that about me,
that there wasn't much to complain of in
my looks; and that's what a girl thinks of
then, and sweethearts, and balls, and all
the other men looking savage when she's
dancing with any one of them. Well, well,
Harry; and what is all this about you and
the young lady your mother has made such
a pet of? Oh, yes, I have my suspicions;
and she's engaged to another man, isn't
she? Your grandfather would have fought
him, I'll be bound; but we live in a peace-
able way now—well, well, no matter; but

hasn't that got something to do with your glum looks, Harry?"

"I tell you, grandmother, I have been hard at work in London. You can't look very brilliant after a few months in London."

"And what keeps you in London at this time of the year?" said this plain-spoken old lady. "Your fancy about getting into the army? Nonsense, man; don't tell me such a tale as that. There's a woman in the case; a Trelyon never put himself so much about from any other cause. To stop in town at this time of the year! Why, your grandfather and your father, too, would have laughed to hear of it. I haven't had a brace of birds or a pheasant sent me since last autumn—not one. Come, sir, be frank with me. I'm an old woman, but I can hold my tongue."

"There's nothing to tell, grandmother," he said. "You just about hit it in that guess of yours—I suppose Juliott told you.

Well, the girl is engaged to another man;
and what more is to be said?"

"The man's in Jamaica?"

"Yes."

"Why are you going down to-day?"

"Only for a brief visit: I've been a long
time away."

The old lady sat silent for some time.
She had heard of the whole affair before;
but she wished to have the rumour con-
firmed. And at first she was sorely troubled
that her grandson should contemplate
marrying an innkeeper's daughter, however
intelligent, amiable, and well-educated the
young lady might be; but she knew the
Trelyons pretty well, and knew that, if he
had made up his mind to it, argument and
remonstrance would be useless. Moreover,
she had a great affection for this young
man, and was strongly disposed to sympa-
thise with any wish of his. She grew in
time to have a great interest in Miss Wenna

Rosewarne; at this moment the chief object of her visit was to make her acquaintance. She grew to pity young Trelyon in his disappointment, and was inclined to believe that the person in Jamaica was something of a public enemy. The fact was, her mere liking for her grandson would have converted her to a sympathy with the wildest project he could have formed.

"Dear, dear," she said, "what awkward things engagements are when they stand in your way. Shall I tell you the truth? I was just about as good as engaged to John Cholmondeley when I gave myself up to your grandfather—but there, when a girl's heart pulls her one way, and her promise pulls her another way, she needs to be a very firm-minded young woman, if she means to hold fast. John Cholmondeley was as good-hearted a young fellow as ever lived—yes, I will say that for him; and I was mightily sorry for him; but—but you

see, that's how things come about. Dear,
dear, that evening at Bath—I remember it
as well as if it was yesterday—and it was
only two months after I had run away with
your grandfather. Yes, there was a ball
that night; and we had kept very quiet, you
know, after coming back; but this time your
grandfather had set his heart on taking me
out before everybody, and you know, he had
to have his way. As sure as I live, Harry,
the first man I saw was John Cholmondeley,
just as white as a ghost—they said he had
been drinking hard and gambling pretty
nearly the whole of these two months. He
wouldn't come near me. He wouldn't take
the least notice of me. The whole night he
pretended to be vastly gay and merry; he
danced with everybody; but his eyes never
came near me. Well, you know what a girl
is—that vexed me a little bit; for there
never was a man such a slave to a woman as
he was to me—dear, dear, the way my father

used to laugh at him, until he got wild with
anger. Well, I went up to him at last,
when he was by himself, and I said to him,
just in a careless way, you know, 'John,
aren't you going to dance with me to-
night?' Well, do you know, his face got
quite white again; and he said—I remember
the very words, all as cold as ice—'Madam,'
says he, 'I am glad to find that your hurried
trip to Scotland has impaired neither your
good looks nor your self-command.' Wasn't
it cruel of him?—but then, poor fellow, he
had been badly used, I admit that. Poor
young fellow, he never did marry; and I
don't believe he ever forgot me to his dying
day. Many a time I'd like to have told him
all about it; and how there was no use in
my marrying him if I liked another man
better; but though we met sometimes,
especially when he came down about the
Reform Bill time—and I do believe I made
a red-hot Radical of him—he was always

very proud, and I hadn't the heart to go back on the old story. But I'll tell you what your grandfather did for him—he got him returned at the very next election, and he on the other side too ; and after a bit a man begins to think more about getting a seat in Parliament than about courting an empty-headed girl. I have met this Mr. Roscorla, haven't I ? "

" Of course you have."

" A good-looking man rather, with a fresh complexion and grey hair ? "

" I don't know what you mean by good looks," said Trelyon, shortly. " I shouldn't think people would call him an Adonis. But there's no accounting for tastes."

" Perhaps I may have been mistaken," the old lady said ; " but there was a gentleman at Plymouth Station who seemed to be something like what I can recall of Mr. Roscorla—you didn't see him, I suppose."

" At Plymouth Station, grandmother ? "

the young man said, becoming rather uneasy.

"Yes. He got into the train just as we
came up. A neatly-dressed man, grey hair,
and a healthy-looking face—I must have
seen him somewhere about here before."

"Roscorla is in Jamaica," said Trelyon,
positively.

Just at this moment the train slowed
into Launceston Station, and the people
began to get out on the platform.

"That is the man I mean," said the old
lady.

Trelyon turned and stared. There, sure
enough, was Mr. Roscorla, looking not one
whit different from the precise, elderly,
fresh-coloured gentleman who had left
Cornwall some seven months before.

"Good Lord, Harry," said the old lady,
nervously looking at her grandson's face,
"don't have a fight here!"

The next second Mr. Roscorla wheeled

round, anxious about some luggage, and now it was his turn to stare in astonishment and anger—anger, because he had been told that Harry Trelyon never came near Cornwall, and his first sudden suspicion was that he had been deceived. All this had happened in a minute. Trelyon was the first to regain his self-command. He walked deliberately forward, held out his hand, and said—

"Hillo, Roscorla; back in England again? I didn't know you were coming."

"No," said Mr. Roscorla, with his face grown just a trifle greyer, "no, I suppose not."

In point of fact he had not informed any one of his coming. He had prepared a little surprise. The chief motive of his return was to get Wenna to cancel for ever that unlucky letter of release he had sent her, which he had done more or less successfully in subsequent correspondence; but he had also hoped to introduce a little roman-

ticism into his meeting with her. He would
enter Eglosilyan on foot. He would wander
down to the rocks at the mouth of the
harbour, on the chance of finding Wenna
there. Might he not hear her humming to
herself, as she sat and sewed, some snatch
of "Your Polly has never been false, she
declares"—or was that the very last ballad
in the world she would now think of singing? Then the delight of regarding again
the placid, bright face and earnest eyes, of
securing once more a perfect understanding
between them, and their glad return to the
inn.

All this had been spoiled by the appearance of this young man : he loved him none
the more for that.

"I suppose you haven't got a trap waiting for you ?" said Trelyon, with cold politeness. "I can drive you over, if you like."

He could do no less than make the offer ;
the other had no alternative but to accept.

Old Mrs. Trelyon heard this compact made with considerable dread.

Indeed, it was a dismal drive over to Eglosilyan, bright as the forenoon was. The old lady did her best to be courteous to Mr. Roscorla and cheerful with her grandson; but she was oppressed by the belief that it was only her presence that had so far restrained the two men from giving vent to the rage and jealousy that filled their hearts. The conversation kept up was singular.

"Are you going to remain in England long, Roscorla?" said the younger of the two men, making an unnecessary cut at one of the two horses he was driving.

"Don't know yet. Perhaps I may."

"Because," said Trelyon, with angry impertinence, "I suppose if you do you'll have to look round for a housekeeper."

The insinuation was felt; and Roscorla's eyes looked anything but pleasant as he answered—

"You forget I've got Mrs. Cornish to look after my house."

"Oh, Mrs. Cornish is not much of a companion for you."

"Men seldom want to make companions of their housekeepers," was the retort, uttered rather hotly.

"But sometimes they wish to have the two offices combined, for economy's sake."

At this juncture Mrs. Trelyon struck in, somewhat wildly, with a remark about an old ruined house, which seemed to have had at one time a private still inside: the danger was staved off for the moment.

"Harry," she said, "mind what you are about; the horses seem very fresh."

"Yes, they like a good run; I suspect they've had precious little to do since I left Cornwall."

Did she fear that the young man was determined to throw them into a ditch or down a precipice, with the wild desire of killing his rival at any cost? If she had known the whole state of affairs between them—the story of the emerald ring, for example—she would have understood at least the difficulty experienced by these two men in remaining decently civil towards each other.

So they passed over the high and wide moors, until far ahead they caught a glimpse of the blue plain of the sea. Mr. Roscorla relapsed into silence; he was becoming a trifle nervous. He was probably so occupied with anticipations of his meeting with Wenna that he failed to notice the objects around him—and one of these, now become visible, was a very handsome young lady, who was coming smartly along a wooded lane, carrying a basket of bright-coloured flowers.

"Why, here's Mabyn Rosewarne. I must wait for her."

Mabyn had seen at a distance Mrs. Tre-

lyon's grey horses; she guessed that the
young master had come back, and that he
had brought some strangers with him   She
did not like to be stared at by strangers.
She came along the path, with her eyes
fixed on the ground; she thought it impertinent of Harry Trelyon to wait to speak
to her.

"Oh, Mabyn," he cried, "you must let
me drive you home ! And let me introduce
you to my grandmother. There is some
one else whom you know.'

The young lady bowed to Mrs. Trelyon ;
then she stared, and changed colour somewhat, when she saw Mr. Roscorla; then she
was helped up into a seat.

"How do you do, Mr. Trelyon?" she
said. "I am very glad to see you have come
back. How do you do, Mr. Roscorla?"

She shook hands with them both, but
not quite in the same fashion.

"And you have sent no message that

you were coming?" she said, looking her companion straight in the face.

"No—no, I did not," he said, angry and embarrassed by the open enmity of the girl. "I thought I should surprise you all——"

"You have surprised me, any way," said Mabyn, "for how can you be so thoughtless? Wenna has been very ill—I tell you, she has been very ill indeed, though she has said little about it, and the least thing upsets her. How can you think of frightening her so? Do you know what you are doing? I wish you would go away back to Launceston, or London, and write her a note there, if you are coming, instead of trying to frighten her!"

This was the language, it appeared to Mr. Roscorla, of a virago; only viragoes do not ordinarily have tears in their eyes, as was the case with Mabyn, when she finished her indignant appeal.

"Mr. Trelyon, do you think it is fair

to go and frighten Wenna so?" she demanded.

"It is none of my business," Trelyon
answered, with an air as if he had said to
his rival, "Yes, go and kill the girl! You
are a nice sort of gentleman, to come down
from London to kill the girl!"

"This is absurd," said Mr. Roscorla,
contemptuously, for he was stung into
reprisal by the persecution of these two;
"a girl isn't so easily frightened out of her
wits. Why, she must have known that my
coming home was at any time probable."

"I have no doubt she feared that it
was," said Mabyn, partly to herself: for
once she was afraid of speaking out.

Presently, however, a brighter light
came over the girl's face.

"Why, I quite forgot," she said,
addressing Harry Trelyon; "I quite forgot
that Wenna was just going up to Trelyon
Hall when I left. Of course, she will be up

there. You will be able to tell her that Mr. Roscorla has arrived, won't you?"

The malice of this suggestion was so apparent that the young gentleman in front could not help grinning at it; fortunately, his face could not be seen by his rival. What *he* thought of the whole arrangement can only be imagined.

And so, as it happened, Mr. Roscorla and his friend Mabyn were dropped at the inn; while Harry Trelyon drove his grandmother up and on to the Hall.

"Well, Harry," the old lady said, "I am glad to be able to breathe at last; I thought you two were going to kill each other."

"There is no fear of that," the young man said; "that is not the way in which this affair has to be settled. It is entirely a matter for her decision—and look how everything is in his favour. I am not even allowed to say a word to her; and even if I could, he is a deal cleverer than me in argument. He would argue my head off in half-an-hour."

"But you don't turn a girl's heart round by argument, Harry. When a girl has to choose between a young lover and an elderly one, it isn't always good sense that directs her choice. Is Miss Wenna Rosewarne at all like her sister?"

"She's not such a tomboy," he said; "but she is quite as straightforward, and proud, and quick to tell you what is the right thing to do. There's no sort of shamming tolerated by these two girls. But then Wenna is gentle, and quieter, and more soft and loveable than Mabyn—in my fancy, you know; and she is more humorous and clever, so that she never gets into those schoolgirl rages. But it is really a shame to compare them like that; and, indeed, if any one said the least thing against one of these girls, the other would precious soon make him regret the day he was born. You don't catch me doing that with either of them; I've had a warning already, when I hinted that Mabyn might probably manage to keep her husband in good order. And so she would, I believe, if the husband were not of the right sort; but when she is really fond of anybody, she becomes their slave out-and-out. There is nothing she wouldn't do for her sister; and her sister thinks there's nobody in the world like Mabyn. So you see——"

He stopped in the middle of this sentence.

" Grandmother," he said, almost in a whisper, " here she is coming along the road."

" Miss Rosewarne ? "

" Yes : shall I introduce you ? "

" If you like."

Wenna was coming down the steep road, between the high hedges, with a small girl on each side of her, whom she was leading by the hand. She was gaily talking to them; you could hear the children laughing at what she said. Old Mrs. Trelyon came to the conclusion that this merry young lady, with the light and free step, the careless talk, and fresh colour in her face, was certainly not dying of any love-affair.

"Take the reins, grandmother, for a minute."

He had leapt down into the road, and was standing before her, almost ere she had time to recognize him. For a moment a quick gleam of gladness shone on her face; then, almost instinctively, she seemed to shrink from him, and she was reserved, distant, and formal.

He introduced her to the old lady, who said something nice to her about her sister. The young man was looking wistfully at her, troubled at heart that she treated him so coldly.

"I have got to break some news to you," he said; "perhaps you will consider it good news."

She looked up quickly.

"Nothing has happened to anybody—only some one has arrived. Mr. Roscorla is at the inn."

She did not flinch. He was vexed with her that she showed no sign of fear or dislike. On the contrary, she quickly said that she must then go down to the inn; and she bade them both good-bye, in a placid and ordinary way; while he drove off, with dark thoughts crowding into his imagination of what might happen down at the inn during the next few days. He was angry with her, he scarcely knew why.

Meanwhile Wenna, apparently quite calm, went on down the road; but there was no more laughing in her voice, no more light in her face.

"Miss Wenna," said the smaller of the

two children, who could not understand
this change, and who looked up with big,
wondering eyes, "why does oo tremble
so?"

CHAPTER V.

When they heard that Wenna was coming down the road they left Mr. Roscorla alone : lovers like to have their meetings and partings unobserved.

She went into the room, pale and yet firm—there was even a sense of gladness in her heart that now she must know the worst. What would he say? How would he receive her? She knew that she was at his mercy.

Well, Mr. Roscorla at this moment was angry enough, for he had been deceived and trifled with in his absence, but he was also anxious, and his anxiety caused him to conceal his anger. He came forward to her with quite a pleasant look on his face; he kissed her and said—

"Why, now, Wenna, how frightened you seem! Did you think I was going to scold you? No, no, no—I hope there is no necessity for that. I am not unreasonable, or over-exacting, as a younger man might be; I can make allowances. Of course I can't say I liked what you told me, when I first heard of it; but then I reasoned with myself: I thought of your lonely position; of the natural liking a girl has for the attention of a young man; of the possibility of any one going thoughtlessly wrong. And really I see no great harm done. A passing fancy—that is all."

"Oh, I hope that is so!" she cried suddenly, with a pathetic earnestness of appeal. "It is so good of you, so generous of you to speak like that!"

For the first time she ventured to raise

her eyes to his face. They were full of gratitude. Mr. Roscorla complimented himself on his knowledge of women; a younger man would have flown into a fury.

"Oh dear, yes, Wenna!" he said lightly, "I suppose all girls have their fancies stray a little bit from time to time; but is there any harm done? None whatever! There is nothing like marriage to fix the affections, as I hope you will discover ere long—the sooner the better, indeed. Now we will dismiss all those unpleasant matters we have been writing about."

"Then you do forgive me? You are not really angry with me?" she said; and then, finding a welcome assurance in his face, she gratefully took his hand and touched it with her lips.

This little act of graceful submission quite conquered Mr. Roscorla, and definitely removed all lingering traces of anger from his heart. He was no longer acting

clemency when he said—with a slight blush
on his forehead :—

"You know, Wenna, I have not been
free from blame either. That letter—it was
merely a piece of thoughtless anger; but
still it was very kind of you to consider it
cancelled and withdrawn when I asked you.
Well, I was in a bad temper at that time.
You cannot look at things so philosophically
when you are far away from home; you feel
yourself so helpless; and you think you are
being unfairly—— However, not another
word! Come, let us talk of all your affairs,
and all the work you have done since I left."

It was a natural invitation; and yet it
revealed in a moment the hollowness of
the apparent reconciliation between them.
What chance of mutual confidence could
there be between these two?

He asked Wenna if she had been busy
in his absence ; and the thought imme-
diately occurred to him that she had had at

least sufficient leisure to go walking about with young Trelyon.

He asked her about the Sewing Club; and she stumbled into the admission that Mr. Trelyon had presented that association with six sewing-machines.

Always Trelyon—always the recurrence of that uneasy consciousness of past events, which divided these two as completely as the Atlantic had done. It was a strange meeting, after that long absence.

"It is a curious thing," he said, rather desperately, "how marriage makes a husband and wife sure of each other. Anxiety is all over then. We have near us, out in Jamaica, several men whose wives and families are here in England; and they accept their exile there as an ordinary commercial necessity. But then they put their whole minds into their work; for they know that when they return to England they will find their wives and families just

as they left them. Of course, in the ma-
jority of cases, the married men there have
taken their wives out with them. Do you
fear a long sea-voyage, Wenna?"

"I don't know," she said, rather
startled.

"You ought to be a good sailor, you
know."

She said nothing to that: she was looking down, dreading what was coming.

"I am sure you must be a good sailor.
I have heard of many of your boating adventures. Weren't you rather fond, some
years ago, of going out at night with the
Lundy pilots?"

"I have never gone a long voyage in a
large vessel," Wenna said, rather faintly.

"But if there was any reasonable object
to be gained, an ordinary sea-voyage would
not frighten you?"

"Perhaps not."

"And they have really very good
steamers going to the West Indies."

" Oh, indeed."

" First-rate! You get a most comfortable cabin."

" I thought you rather—in your description of it—in your first letter——"

" Oh," said he, hurriedly and lightly (for he had been claiming sympathy on account of the discomfort of his voyage out), " perhaps I made a little too much of that. Besides, I did not make a proper choice in time. One gains experience in such matters. Now, if you were going out to Jamaica, I should see that you had every comfort."

" But you don't wish me to go out to Jamaica?" she said, almost retreating from him.

" Well," said he, with a smile, for his only object at present was to familiarize her with the idea, " I don't particularly wish it, unless the project seemed a good one to you. You see, Wenna, I find that my stay there must be longer than I expected. When I went out at first the intention of my partners and myself was that I should merely be on the spot to help our manager by agreeing his accounts at the moment, and undertaking a lot of work of that sort, which otherwise would have consumed time in correspondence. I was merely to see the whole thing well started, and then return. But now I find that my superintendence may be needed there for a long while. Just when everything promises so well, I should not like to imperil all our chances simply for a year or two."

" Oh no, of course not," Wenna said : she had no objection to his remaining in Jamaica for a year or two longer than he had intended.

" That being so," he continued, " it occurred to me that perhaps you might consent to our marriage before I leave England again ; and that, indeed, you might

even make up your mind to try a trip to
Jamaica. Of course, we should have considerable spells of holiday, if you thought it
was worth while coming home for a short
time. I assure you, you would find the
place delightful—far more delightful than
anything I told you in my letters, for I'm
not very good at describing things. And
there is a fair amount of society."

He did not prefer the request in an
impassioned manner. On the contrary, he
merely felt that he was satisfying himself
by carrying out an intention he had formed
on his voyage home. If, he had said to
himself, Wenna and he became friends,
he would at least suggest to her that she
might put an end to all further suspense
and anxiety by at once marrying him and
accompanying him to Jamaica.

"What do you say?" he said, with a
friendly smile. "Or have I frightened you
too much? Well, let us drop the subject
altogether for the present."

Wenna breathed again.

"Yes," said he, good-naturedly, "you can think over it. In the mean time do not harass yourself about that or anything else. You know, I have come home to spend a holiday."

"And won't you come and see the others?" said Wenna, rising, with a glad look of relief on her face.

"Oh yes, if you like," he said; and then he stopped short, and an angry gleam shot into his eyes.

"Wenna, who gave you that ring?"

"Oh, Mabyn did," was the frank reply; but all the same Wenna blushed hotly, for that matter of the emerald ring had not been touched upon.

"Mabyn did?" he repeated, somewhat suspiciously. "She must have been in a generous mood."

"When you know Mabyn as well as I do, you will find out that she always is," said Miss Wenna, quite cheerfully; she was indeed in the best of spirits to find that this dreaded interview had not been so very frightful after all, and that she had done no mortal injury to one who had placed his happiness in her hands.

When Mr. Roscorla, some time after, set out to walk by himself up to Basset Cottage, whither his luggage had been sent before him, he felt a little tired. He was not accustomed to violent emotions; and that morning he had gone through a good deal. His anger and anxiety had for long been fighting for mastery; and both had reached their climax that morning. On the one hand, he wished to avenge himself for the insult paid him, and to show that he was not to be trifled with; on the other hand, his anxiety lest he should be unable to make up matters with Wenna, led him to put an unusual value upon her. What was the result, now that he had definitely won

her back to himself? What was the sentiment that followed on these jarring emotions of the morning ?

To tell the truth, a little disappointment.
Wenna was not looking her best when she
entered the room ; even now he remembered
that the pale face rather shocked him. She
was more—insignificant, perhaps, is the best
word—than he had expected. Now that he
had got back the prize which he thought he
had lost, it did not seem to him, after all, to
be so wonderful.

And in this mood he went up and walked
into the pretty little cottage which had once
been his home. "What?" he said to himself, looking in amazement at the small old-
fashioned parlour, and at the still smaller
study, filled with books, "is it possible
that I ever proposed to myself to live and
die in a hole like this?—my only companion
a cantankerous old fool of a woman, my only
occupation reading the newspapers, my only
society the good folks of the inn ?"

He thanked God he had escaped. His knocking about the world for a bit had opened up his mind. The possibility of his having in time a handsome income had let in upon him many new and daring ambitions.

His housekeeper, having expressed her grief that she had just posted some letters to him, not knowing that he was returning to England, brought in a number of small passbooks and a large sheet of blue paper.

" If yü bain't too tired, zor, vor to look over the accounts, 'tis all theear but the pultry that Mr.——"

" Good heavens, Mrs. Cornish ! " said he, " do you think I am going to look over a lot of grocers' bills ? "

Mrs. Cornish not only hinted in very plain language that her master had been at one time particular enough about grocers bills, and all other bills, however trifling, but further proceeded to give him a full and minute account of the various incidental expenses to which she had been put through young Penny Luke having broken a window by flinging a stone from the road; through the cat having knocked down the best tea-pot; through the pig having got out of its sty, gone mad, and smashed a cucumber-frame; and so forth, and so forth. In desperation, Mr. Roscorla got up, put on his hat, and went outside, leaving her at once astonished and indignant over his want of interest in what at one time had been his only care.

Was this, then, the place in which he had chosen to spend the rest of his life, without change, without movement, without interest? It seemed to him at the moment a living tomb. There was not a human being within sight. Far away out there lay the grey-blue sea—a plain without a speck on it. The great black crags at the mouth of the harbour were voiceless and sterile;

could anything have been more bleak than the bare uplands on which the pale sun of an English October was shining? The quiet crushed him; there was not a nigger near to swear at; nor could he, at the impulse of a moment, get on horseback and ride over to the busy and interesting and picturesque scene supplied by his faithful coolies at work.

What was he to do on this very first day in England, for example? Unpack his luggage, in which were some curiosities he had brought home for Wenna?—there was too much trouble in that. Walk about the garden and smoke a pipe as had been his wont?—he had got emancipated from these delights of dotage. Attack his grocers' bills?—he swore by all his gods that he would have nothing to do with the price of candles and cheese now or at any future time. The return of the exile to his native land had already produced a feeling of deep disappointment; when he married, he said to himself, he would take very good care not to sink into an oyster-like life in Eglosilyan.

About a couple of hours after, however, he was reminded that Eglosilyan had its small measure of society, by the receipt of a letter from Mrs. Trelyon, who said she had just heard of his arrival, and hastened to ask him whether he would dine at the Hall not next evening but the following one, to meet two old friends of his, General and Lady Weekes, who were there on a brief visit.

"And I have written to ask Miss Rosewarne," Mrs. Trelyon continued, "to spare us the same evening, so that we hope to have you both. Perhaps you will kindly add your entreaties to mine."

The friendly intention of this postscript was evident; and yet it did not seem to please Mr. Roscorla. This Sir Percy

Weekes had been a friend of his father's; and when the younger Roscorla was a young man about town, Lady Weekes had been very kind to him, and had nearly got him married once or twice. There was a great contrast between those days and these. He hoped the old General would not be tempted to come and visit him at Basset Cottage.

"Oh, Wenna," said he carelessly, to her next morning, "Mrs. Trelyon told me she had asked you to go up there to-morrow evening."

"Yes," Wenna said, looking rather uncomfortable. Then she added, quickly, "Would it displease you if I did not go? I ought to be at a children's party at Mr. Trewhella's."

This was precisely what Mr. Roscorla wanted; but he said—

"You must not be shy, Wenna. However, please yourself; you need have no fear

of vexing me. But I must go; for the
Weekeses are old friends of mine."

· "They stayed at the inn two or three
days in May last," said Wenna, innocently.
" They came here by chance and found
Mrs. Trelyon from home."

Mr. Roscorla seemed startled.

"Oh," said he. " Did they—did they
—ask for me ? "

" Yes, I believe they did," Wenna said.

" Then you told them," said Mr. Roscorla, with a pleasant smile, " you told
them, of course, why you were the best
person in the world to give them information about me ? "

" Oh, dear, no," said Wenna, blushing
hotly, " they spoke to Jennifer."

Mr. Roscorla felt himself rebuked. It
was George Rosewarne's express wish that
his daughters should not be approached by
strangers visiting the inn as if they were
officially connected with the place : Mr.

Roscorla should have remembered that inquiries would be made of a servant.

But, as it happened, Sir Percy and his wife had really made the acquaintance of both Wenna and Mabyn on their chance visit to Eglosilyan; and it was of these two girls they were speaking when Mr. Roscorla was announced in Mrs. Trelyon's drawing-room the following evening. The thin, wiry, white-moustached old man, who had wonderfully bright eyes and a great vivacity of spirits for a veteran of seventy-four, was standing in front of the fire, and declaring to everybody that two such well-accomplished, smart, talkative, and ladylike young women he had never met with in his life.

" What did you say the name was, my dear Mrs. Trelyon? Rosewarne, eh?— Rosewarne? A good old Cornish name— as good as yours, Roscorla. So they're called Rosewarne—Gad, if her august lady-

ship there wants to appoint a successor,
I'm willing to let her choice fall on one
o' these two girls."

Her august ladyship—a dark and silent
old woman of eighty—did not like, in the
first place, to be called her august ladyship,
and did not relish either having her death
talked of as a joke.

" Roscorla, now—Roscorla—there's a
good chance for you, eh?" continued the
old General. "We never could get you
married, you know—wild young dog. Don't
ye know the girls?"

" Oh yes, Sir Percy," Mr. Roscorla said,
with no great good will; then he turned to
the fire and began to warm his hands.

There was a tall young gentleman standing there who, in former days, would have
been delighted to cry out on such an occasion, " Why, Roscorla's going to marry one
of 'em." He remained silent now.

He was very silent, too, throughout the

evening ; and almost anxiously civil towards
Mr. Roscorla. He paid great attention
when the latter was describing to the company at table the beauties of West Indian
scenery, the delights of West Indian life,
the change that had come over the prospects
of Jamaica since the introduction of coolie
labour, and the fashion in which the rich
merchants of Cuba were setting about getting plantations there for the growth of
tobacco. Mr. Roscorla spoke with the air
of a man who now knew what the world
was. When the old General asked him if
he were coming back to live in Eglosilyan
after he had become a millionaire, he
laughed, and said that one's coffin came
soon enough without one's rushing to meet
it. No ; when he came back to England
finally, he would live in London ; and had
Sir Percy still that old walled-in house in
Brompton ?

Sir Percy paid less heed to these

descriptions of Jamaica than Harry Trelyon did, for his next neighbour was old Mrs. Trelyon, and these two venerable flirts were talking of old acquaintances and old times at Bath and Cheltenham, and of the celebrated beauties, wits, and murderers of other days, in a manner which her silent ladyship did not at all seem to approve. The General was bringing out all his old-fashioned gallantry—compliments, easy phrases in French, polite attentions; his companion began to use her fan with a coquettish grace, and was vastly pleased when a reference was made to her celebrated flight to Gretna Green.

"Ah, Sir Percy," she said, "the men were men in those days, and the women women, I promise you; no beating about the bush, but the fair word given, and the fair word taken; and then a broken head for whoever should interfere, father, uncle, or brother, no matter who; and you know our family, Sir Percy, our family were among the worst——"

"I tell you what, madam," said the General, hotly, "your family had among 'em the handsomest women in the west of England—and the handsomest men, too, by Gad! Do you remember Jane Swanhope— the Fair Maid of Somerset they used to call her—that married the fellow living down Yeovil way, who broke his neck in a steeplechase?"

"Do I remember her," said the old lady. "She was one of my bridesmaids when they took me up to London to get married properly after I came back! She was my cousin on the mother's side; but they were connected with the Trelyons, too. And do you remember old John Trelyon of Polkerris; and did you ever see a man straighter in the back than he was, at seventy-one, when he married his second wife—that was at Exeter, I think. But

there now, you don't find such men and
women in these times; and do you know
the reason of that, Sir Percy? I'll tell
you; it's the doctors. The doctors can
keep all the sickly ones alive now; before it
was only the strong ones that lived. Dear,
dear me, when I hear some of those London
women talk—it is nothing but a catalogue
of illnesses and diseases. No wonder they
should say in church, 'There is no health
in us;' everyone of them has something
the matter, even the young girls, poor
things; and pretty mothers they're likely
to make! They're a misery to themselves;
they'll bring miserable things into the
world; and all because the doctors have
become so clever in pulling sickly people
through. That's my opinion, Sir Percy.
The doctors are responsible for five-sixths
of all the suffering you hear of in families,
either through illness or the losing of one's
friends and relatives."

"Upon my word, madam," the General protested, "you use the doctor badly. He is blamed if he kills people, and he is blamed if he keeps them alive. What is he to do?"

"Do? He can't help saving the sickly ones now," the old lady admitted; "for relatives will have it done, and they know he can do it; but it's a great misfortune, Sir Percy, that's what it is, to have all these sickly creatures growing up to inter-marry into the good old families that used to be famous for their comeliness and strength. There was a man, yes, I remember him well, that came from Devon-shire—he was a man of good family, too, and they made such a noise about his wrestling. Said I to myself, wrestling is not a fit amusement for gentlemen, but if this man comes up to our country, there's one or other of the Trelyons will try his mettle. And well I remember saying to my eldest son George—you remember when he was a young man, Sir Percy, no older than his own son there—'George,' I said, 'if this Mr. So-and-so comes into these parts, mind you have nothing to do with him; for wrestling is not fit for gentlemen.' 'All right, mother,' said he; but he laughed, and I knew what the laugh meant. My dear Sir Percy, I tell you the man hadn't a chance—I heard of it all afterwards. George caught him up, before he could begin any of his tricks, and flung him on to the hedge—and there were a dozen more in our family who could have done it, I'll be bound."

"But then, you know, Mrs. Trelyon," Mr. Roscorla ventured to say, "physical strength is not everything that is needed. If the doctors were to let the sickly ones die, we might be losing all sorts of great poets, and statesmen, and philosophers."

The old lady turned on him.

"And do you think a man has to be sickly to be clever? No, no, Mr. Roscorla, give him better health and you give him a better head, that's what we believed in the old days. I fancy, now, there were greater men before all this coddling began than there are now, yes, I do; and if there is a great man coming into the world, the chances are just as much that he'll be among the strong ones as among the sickly ones—what do you think, Sir Percy?"

"I declare you're right, madam," said he, gallantly. "You've quite convinced me. Of course, some of 'em must go—I say, let the sickly ones go."

"I never heard such brutal, such murderous sentiments expressed in my life before," said a solemn voice; and every one became aware that at last Lady Weekes had spoken. Her speech was the signal for universal silence, in the midst of which the ladies got up and left the room.

Trelyon took his mother's place, and sent round the wine. He was particularly attentive to Mr. Roscorla, who was surprised. "Perhaps," thought the latter, "he is anxious to atone for all this bother that is now happily over."

If the younger man was silent and preoccupied, that was not the case with Mr. Roscorla, who was already assuming the airs of a rich person and speaking of his being unable to live in this district or that district of London, just as. if he expected to purchase a lease of Buckingham Palace on his return from Jamaica.

"And how are all my old friends in Hans Place, Sir Percy!" he cried.

"You've been a deserter, sir, you've been a deserter for many a year now," the General said gaily, "but we're all willing to have you back again, to a quiet rubber after dinner, you know. Do you remember old John Thwaites? Ah, he's gone now—left 150,000*l.* to build a hospital, and only 5,000*l.* to his sister. The poor old woman believed some one would marry her when she got the whole of her brother's money—so I'm told—and when the truth became known, what did she do? Gad, sir, she wrote a novel abusing her own brother. By the way, that reminds me of a devilish good thing I heard when I was here last—down at the inn, you know—what's the name of the girls I was talking about? Well, her ladyship caught one of them reading a novel, and not very well pleased with it, and says she to the young lady, 'Don't you like that book?' Then says the girl—let me see what was it?—Gad, I must go and ask her ladyship——"

And off he trotted to the drawing-room. He came back in a couple of minutes.

"Of course," said he. "Devilish stupid of me to forget it. 'Why?' said the young lady, 'I think the author has been trying to keep the second commandment, for there's nothing in the book that has any likeness to anything in heaven above, or in the earth beneath, or the heavens under the earth——"

" The waters under the earth."

" I mean the waters, of course. Gad, her ladyship was immensely tickled."

" Which of the two young ladies was it, Sir Percy? The younger, I suppose?" said Mr. Roscorla.

" No, no, the elder sister, of course," said Trelyon.

" Yes, the elder one it was—the quiet one—and an uncommon nice girl she is. Well, there's Captain Walters—the old sea dog—still to the fore; and his uniform too —don't you remember the uniform with the red cuffs that hasn't been seen in the navy for a couple of centuries, I should think! His son's got into Parliament now—gone over to the Rads, and the working-men, and

those fellows that are scheming to get the
land divided among themselves—all in the
name of philosophy—and it's a devilish fine
sort of philosophy, that is, when you haven't
a rap in your pocket, and when you prove
that everybody who has must give it up.
He came to my house the other day, and
he was jawing away about Primogeniture,
and Entail, and Direct Taxation, and equal
electoral districts, and I don't know what
besides. 'Walters,' said I, ' Walters, you've
got nothing to share, and so you don't mind
a general division. When you have, you'll
want to stick to what's in your own pocket.'
Had him there, eh?"

The old general beamed and laughed
over his smartness; he was conscious of
having said something that, in shape at
least, was like an epigram.

"I must rub up my acquaintance in
that quarter," said Roscorla, "before I
leave again. Fortunately, I have always

kept up my club subscription ; and you'll come and dine with me, Sir Percy, won't you, when I get to town ? "

" Are you going to town ? " said Trelyon quickly.

" Oh, yes, of course."

" When ? "

The question was abrupt, and it made Roscorla look at the young man as he answered. Trelyon seemed to him to be very much harassed about something or other.

" Well, I suppose in a week or so ; I am only home for a holiday, you know."

" Oh, you'll be here for a week ? " said the young man, submissively. " When do you think of returning to Jamaica ? "

" Probably at the beginning of next month. Fancy leaving England in November—just at the most hideous time of the year—and in a week or two getting out into summer again, with the most beautiful climate, and foliage, and what not, all around you! I can tell you a man makes a great mistake who settles down to a sort of vegetable life anywhere—you don't catch me at that again."

"There's some old women," observed the General, who was so anxious to show his profundity that he quite forgot the invidious character of the comparison, "who are just like trees—as much below the ground as above it—isn't that true, eh? They're a deal more at home among the people they have buried than among those that are alive. I don't say that's your case, Roscorla. You're comparatively a young man yet—you've got brisk health—I don't wonder at your liking to knock about. 'As for you, young Trelyon, what do you mean to do?"

Harry Trelyon started.

"Oh," said he, with some confusion, "I have no immediate plans. Yes, I have—

don't you know I have been cramming for the Civil Service examinations for first commissions ? "

"And what the devil made the War Office go to those civilians?" muttered the General.

"And if I pull through, I shall want all your influence to get me gazetted to a good regiment. Don't they often shunt you on to the First or Second West Indians?"

"And you've enough money to back you too," said the General. "I tell you what it is, gentlemen, if they abolish the purchase of commissions in the army—and they're always talking about it—they don't know what they'll bring about. They'll have two sets of officers in the army—men with money, who like a good mess, and live far beyond their pay, and men with no money at all, who've got to live on their pay, and how can they afford the regimental mess out of that? But Parliament won't stand it you'll see. The War Minister 'll be beaten if he brings it on— take my word for that."

The old General had probably never heard of a royal warrant and its mighty powers.

"So you're going to be one of us?" he said to Trelyon. "Well, you've a smart figure for a uniform. You're the first of your side of the family to go into the army, eh? You had some naval men among you, eh?"

"I think you'd better ask my grandmother," said young Trelyon, with a laugh; "she'll tell you stories about 'em by the hour together."

"She's a wonderful woman that—a wonderful old creature," said the General, just as if he were a sprightly young fellow talking of the oldest inhabitant of the district. "She's not one of them that are half buried; she's wide enough awake, I'll be bound. Gad, what a handsome woman she was when I saw her first. Well, lads, let's join the ladies; I'm none of your steady-going old topers. Enough's as good's a feast—that's my motto. And I can't write my name on a slate with my knuckles, either."

And so they went into the large, dimly-'lit, red chamber, where the women were having tea round the blazing fire. The men took various chairs about; the conversation became general; old Lady Weekes feebly endeavoured to keep up her eyelids. In about half-an-hour or so Mrs. Trelyon happened to glance round the room. .

" Where's Harry? " said she.

No one apparently had noticed that Master Harry had disappeared.

CHAPTER VI.

A DARK CONSPIRACY.

Now, when Harry Trelyon drove up to the Hall, after leaving Wenna Rosewarne in the road, he could not tell why he was vexed with her. He imagined somehow that she should not have allowed Mr. Roscorla to come home—and to come home just at this moment, when he, Trelyon, had stolen down for a couple of days to have a shy look at the sweetheart who was so far out of his reach. She ought to have been alone. Then she ought not to have looked so calm and complacent on going away to meet Mr. Roscorla; she ought to have been afraid. She ought to have—in short everything was wrong, and Wenna was largely to blame.

"Well, grandmother," said he, as they drove through the avenue, "don't you expect every minute to flush a covey of parsons?"

He was angry with Wenna; and so he broke out once more in his old vein.

"There are worse men than the parsons, Harry," the old lady said.

"I'll bet you a sovereign there are two on the doorstep."

He would have lost. There was not a clergyman of any sort in or about the house.

"Isn't Mr. Barnes here?" said he to his mother.

Mrs. Trelyon flushed slightly, as she said—

"No, Harry, Mr. Barnes is not here. Nor is he likely to visit here again."

Now Mr. Roscorla would at once have

perceived what a strange little story lay behind that simple speech; but Mr. Harry, paying no attention to it, merely said he was heartily glad to hear of it, and showed his gratitude by being unusually polite to his mother during the rest of his stay.

"And so Mr. Roscorla has come back," his mother said. "General Weekes was asking about him only yesterday. We must see if he will come up to dinner the night after to-morrow——and Miss Rose-warne also."

"You may ask her—you ought to ask her—but she won't come," said he.

"How do you know?" Mrs. Trelyon said, with a gentle wonder. "She has been here very often of late."

"Have you let her walk up?"

"No, I have generally driven down for her when I wanted to see her; and the way she has been working for these people is extraordinary—never tired, always cheerful, ready to be bothered by anybody, and patient with their suspicions and simplicity, beyond belief. I am sure Mr. Roscorla will have an excellent wife."

"I am not at all sure that he will," said her son, goaded past endurance.

"Why, Harry," said his mother, with her eyes wide open, "I thought you had a great respect for Miss Rosewarne."

"I have," he said, abruptly,—"far too great a respect to like the notion of her marrying that old fool."

"Would you rather not have him to dinner?"

"Oh, I should like to have him to dinner."

For one evening, at least, this young man considered, these two would be separated. He was pretty sure that Roscorla would come to meet General Weekes; he was positive that Wenna would not come to the house while he himself was in it.

But the notion that, except during this one evening, his rival would have free access to the inn, and would spend pleasant hours there, and would take Wenna with him for walks along the coast, maddened him. He dared not go down to the village, for fear of seeing these two together. He walked about the grounds, or went away over to the cliffs, torturing his heart with imagining Roscorla's opportunities. And once or twice he was on the point of going straight down to Eglosilyan, and calling on Wenna, before Roscorla's face, to be true to her own heart, and declare herself free from this old and hateful entanglement.

In these circumstances, his grandmother was not a good companion for him. In her continual glorification of the self-will of the Trelyons, and her stories of the wild deeds she had done, she was unconsciously driving him to some desperate thing, against his better judgment.

"Why, grandmother," he said, one day, "you hint that I am a nincompoop because I don't go and carry off that girl and marry her against her will.   Is that what you mean by telling me of what the men did in former days?   Well, I can tell you this, that it would be a deal easier for me to try that than not to try it.   The difficulty is in holding your hand.   But what good would you do, after all?   The time has gone by for that sort of thing.   I shouldn't like to have on my hands a woman sulking because she was married by force—besides, you can't do these mad freaks now — there are too many police-courts about."

"By force?   No!" the old lady said. "The girls I speak of were as glad to run away as the men, I can tell you, and they did it, too, when their relations were against the match."

"Of course, if both he and she are agreed, the way is as smooth now as it was then; you don't need to care much for relations."

"But Harry, you don't know what a girl thinks," this dangerous old lady said. "She has her notions of duty, and her respect for her parents, and all that; and if the man only went and reasoned with her, he would never carry the day; but just as she comes out of a ball-room some night, when she is all aglow with fun and pleasure, and ready to become romantic with the stars, you see, and the darkness, then just show her a carriage, a pair of horses, a marriage license, and her own maid to accompany her, and see what will happen! Why, she'll hop into the carriage like a dicky bird; then she'll have a bit of a cry; and then she'll recover, and be mad with the delight of escaping from those behind her. That's how to win a girl, man! The sweethearts of these days think too much, that's about it: it's all done by argument between them."

"You're a wicked old woman, grandmother," said Trelyon, with a laugh. "You oughtn't to put such notions into the head of a well-conducted young man like me."

"Well, you're not such a booby as you used to be, Harry," the old lady admitted. "Your manners are considerably improved, and there was much room for improvement. You're growing a good deal like your grandfather."

"But there's no Gretna Green now-a-days," said Trelyon, as he went outside, "so you can't expect me to be perfect, grandmother."

On the first night of his arrival at Eglosilyan he stole away in the darkness, down to the inn. There were no lamps in the steep road which was rendered all the darker by the high rocky bank with its rough masses of foliage; he feared that by accident some one might be out and meet him. But in the absolute silence, under the stars, he made his way down until he was near the inn; and there in the black shadow of the road, he stood and looked at the lighted windows. Roscorla was doubtless within—lying in an easy-chair, probably, by the fire, while Wenna sang her old-fashioned songs to him. He would assume the air of being one of the family now—only holding himself a little above the family. Perhaps he was talking of the house he meant to take when he and Wenna married.

That was no wholesome food for reflection on which this young man's mind was now feeding. He stood there in the darkness, himself white as a ghost, while all the vague imaginings of what might be going on within the house seemed to be eating at his heart. This, then, was the comfort he had found, by secretly stealing away from London for a day or two; he had arrived just in time to find his rival triumphant.

The private door of the inn was at this moment opened; a warm glow of yellow streamed out into the darkness.

" Good-night," said some one : was it Wenna?

" Good-night," was the answer; and then the figure of a man passed down the road.

Trelyon breathed more freely; at last his rival was out of the house. Wenna was now alone; would she go up into her own room, and think over all the events of the day? And would she remember that he had come to Eglosilyan; and that she could, if any such feeling arose in her heart, summon him at need?

It was very late that night before Trelyon returned—he had gone all round by the harbour, and the cliffs, and the high-lying church on the hill. All in the house had gone to bed; but there was a fire burning in his study; and there were biscuits and wine on the table. A box of cigars stood on the mantelpiece.

Apparently he was in no mood for the indolent comfort thus suggested. He stood for a minute or two before the fire, staring into it, and seeing other things than the flaming coals there; then he moved about the room, in an impatient and excited fashion; finally, with his hand trembling a little bit, he sat down and wrote this note :—

" Dear Mother,

" The horses and carriage will be at Launceston station by the first train on Saturday morning. Will you please send Jakes over for them? And bid him take the horses up to Mr. ——'s stables, and have them fed, watered, and properly rested before he drives them over.

" Your affectionate son,
" Harry Trelyon."

Next morning, as Mabyn Rosewarne was coming briskly up the Trevenna road carrying in her arms a pretty big parcel, she was startled by the appearance of a young man, who suddenly showed himself overhead, and then scrambled down the rocky bank until he stood beside her.

" I've been watching for you all the morning, Mabyn," said Trelyon. " I——I want to speak to you. Where are you going?"

" Up to Mr. Trewhella's. You know his granddaughter is very nearly quite well again; and there is to be a great gathering of children there to-night to celebrate her recovery. This is a cake I am carrying that Wenna has made herself."

" Is Wenna to be there?" Trelyon said, eagerly.

" Why, of course," said Mabyn, petulantly. " What do you think the children could do without her?"

"Look here, Mabyn," he said. "I want to speak to you very particularly. Couldn't you just as well go round by the farm road? Let me carry your cake for you."

Mabyn guessed what he wanted to speak about, and willingly made the circuit by a more private road leading by one of the upland farms. At a certain point they came to a stile; and here they rested. So far Trelyon had said nothing of consequence.

"Oh, do you know, Mr. Trelyon," Mabyn remarked, quite innocently, "I have been reading such a nice book—all about Jamaica."

"So you're interested about Jamaica, too?" said he, rather bitterly.

"Yes, much. Do you know that it is the most fearful place for storms in the whole world—the most awful hurricanes that come smashing down everything and killing people. You can't escape if you're in the way of the hurricane. It whirls the roofs off the houses, and twists out the plantain trees just like straws. The rivers wash away whole acres of canes and swamp the farms. Sometimes the sea rages so that boats are carried right up into the streets of Kingston. There!"

"But why does that please you?"

"Why," she said, with proud indignation, "the notion of people talking as if they could go out to Jamaica and live for ever, and come back just when they please—it is too ridiculous! Many accidents may happen. And isn't November a very bad time for storms? Ships often get wrecked going out to the West Indies, don't they?"

At another time Trelyon would have laughed at this bloodthirsty young woman; at this moment he was too serious.

"Mabyn," said he, "I can't bear this

any longer—standing by like a fool and looking on while another man is doing his best to marry Wenna : I can't go on like this any longer. Mabyn, when did you say she would leave Mr. Trewhella's house to-night?"

"I did not say anything about it. I suppose we shall leave about ten ; the young ones leave at nine."

"You will be there?"

"Yes, Wenna and I are to keep order."

"Nobody else with you?"

"No."

He looked at her rather hesitatingly.

"And supposing, Mabyn," he said slowly, "supposing you and Wenna were to leave at ten, and that it is a beautiful clear night, you might walk down by the wood instead of by the road; and then, supposing that you came out on the road down at the foot, and you found there a carriage and pair of horses——"

Mabyn began to look alarmed.

"And if I was there," he continued, more rapidly, "and I said to Wenna suddenly, 'Now Wenna, think nothing, but come and save yourself from this marriage! Here is your sister will come with you—and I will drive you to Plymouth——'"

"Oh, Mr. Trelyon!" Mabyn cried, with a sudden joy in her face, "she would do it! She would do it!"

"And you, would you come too?" he demanded.

"Yes!" the girl cried, full of excitement. "And then, Mr. Trelyon, and then?"

"Why," he cried boldly, "up to London at once—twenty-four hours' start of everybody—and in London we are safe! Then, you know, Mabyn——"

"Yes, yes, Mr. Trelyon!"

"Don't you think now that we two could persuade her to a quick marriage—

with a special license, you know—you could persuade her, I am sure, Mabyn——"

In the gladness of her heart Mabyn felt herself at this moment ready to fall on the young man's neck and kiss him. But she was a properly conducted young person; and so she rose from the big block of slate on which she had been sitting and managed to suppress any great intimation of her abounding joy. But she was very proud, all the same; and there was a great firmness about her lips as she said :—

"We will do it, Mr. Trelyon; we will do it. Do you know why Wenna submits to this engagement? Because she reasons with her conscience, and persuades herself that it is right. When you meet her like that, she will have no time to consider——"

" That is precisely what my grandmother says," Trelyon said, with a triumphant laugh.

" Yes, she was a girl once," Mabyn

replied, sagely. " Well, well, tell me all about it ! What arrangements have you made ?   You haven't got the special license ? "

" No," said he, " I didn't make up my mind to try this on till last night. But the difference of a day is nothing, when you are with her. We shall be able to hide ourselves away pretty well in London, don't you think ? "

" Of course ! " cried Mabyn, confidently. " But tell me more, Mr. Trelyon ! What have you arranged ? What have you done ? "

" What could I do until I knew whether you'd help me ? "

" You must bring a fearful amount of wraps with you."

" Certainly—more than you'll want, I know. And I shan't light the lamps until I hear you coming along; for they would attract attention down in the valley. I should like to wait for you elsewhere; but if I did that you couldn't get Wenna to come with you. Do you think you will even then?"

"Oh yes," said Mabyn cheerfully. "Nothing easier! I shall tell her she's afraid; and then she would walk down the face of Black Cliff. By the way, Mr. Trelyon, I must bring something to eat with me, and some wine—she will be so nervous —and the long journey will tire her."

"You will be at Mr. Trewhella's, Mabyn; you can't go carrying things about with you!"

"I could bring a bit of cake in my pocket," Mabyn suggested; but this seemed even to her so ludicrous that she blushed and laughed and agreed that Mr. Trelyon should bring the necessary provisions for the wild night-ride to Plymouth.

"Oh, it does so please me to think of it!" she said with a curious anxious excitement as well as gladness in her face; "I hope I have not forgotten to arrange anything. Let me see—we start at ten: then down through the wood to the road in the hollow—oh. I hope there will be nobody coming along just then!—then you light the lamps—then you come forward to persuade Wenna—by the way, Mr. Trelyon. where must I go? Shall I not be dreadfully in the way?"

"You? You must stand by the horses' heads! I shan't have my man with me. And yet they're not very fiery animals—they'll be less fiery. the unfortunate wretches. when they get to Plymouth."

"At what time?"

"About half past three in the morning. if we go straight on," said he.

"Do you know a good hotel there?" said the practical Mabyn.

"The best one is by the station: but if you sleep in the front of the house, you have the whistling of engines all night long, and if you sleep in the back, you overlook a barracks, and the confounded trumpeting begins about four o'clock, I believe."

"Wenna and I won't mind that—we shall be too tired," Mabyn said, "Do you think they could give us a little hot coffee when we arrive?"

"Oh yes! I'll give the night-porter a sovereign a cup—then he'll offer to bring it to you in buckets. Now don't you think the whole thing is beautifully arranged, Mabyn?"

"It is quite lovely!" the girl said joyously, "for we shall be off with the morning train to London, while Mr. Roscorla is pottering about Launceston station at mid-day! Then we must send a telegram from Plymouth, a fine dramatic telegram; and my father, he will swear a little, but be quite content, and my mother—do you know, Mr. Trelyon, I believe my mother will be as glad as anybody! What shall we say?—' *To Mr. Rosewarne, Eglosilyan. We have fled. Not the least good pursuing us. May as well make up your mind to the inevitable. Will write to-morrow.*' Is that more than the twenty words for a shilling?"

"We shan't grudge the other shilling if it is," the young man said. "Now you must go on with your cake, Mabyn! I am off to see after the horses' shoes. Mind, as soon after ten as you can—just where the path from the wood comes into the main road."

Then she hesitated, and for a second or two she remained thoughtful and silent; while he was inwardly hoping that she was not going to draw back. Suddenly she looked up at him, with earnest and anxious eyes.

"Oh, Mr. Trelyon," she said, "this is a very serious thing. You—you will be kind to our Wenna after she is married to you!"

"You will see, Mabyn," he answered gently.

"You don't know how sensitive she is," she continued, apparently thinking over all the possibilities of the future in a much graver fashion than she had done. "If you were unkind to her, it would kill her. Are you quite sure you won't regret it?"

"Yes, I am quite sure of that,"said he, "as sure as a man may be. I don't think you need fear my being unkind to Wenna. Why, what has put such thoughts into your head?"

"If you were to be cruel to her or indifferent," she said, slowly and absently, "I know that would kill her. But I know more than that. *I would kill you.*"

"Mabyn," he said, quite startled, "whatever has put such thoughts into your head?"

"Why," she said, passionately, "haven't I seen already how a man can treat her?

Haven't I read the insolent letters he has sent her? Haven't I seen her throw herself on her bed, beside herself with grief? And—and—these are things I don't forget, Mr. Trelyon. No, I have got a word to say to Mr. Roscorla yet for his treatment of my sister—and I will say it. And then——"

The proud lips were beginning to quiver.

"Come, come, Mabyn," said Trelyon, gently, "don't imagine all men are the same. And perhaps Roscorla will have been paid out quite sufficiently when he hears of to-night's work. I shan't bear him any malice after that, I know. Already, I confess, I feel a good deal of compunction as regards him."

"I don't at all—I don't a bit," said Mabyn, who very quickly recovered herself whenever Mr. Roscorla's name was mentioned. "If you only can get her to go away with you, Mr. Trelyon, it will serve him just right. Indeed, it is on his account that I hope you will be successful. I—I don't quite like Wenna running away with you, to tell you the truth—I would rather have her left to a quiet decision, and to a marriage with everybody approving. But there is no chance of that. This is the only thing that will save her."

"That is precisely what I said to you," Trelyon said, eagerly, for he was afraid of losing so invaluable an ally.

"And you will be very, *very* kind to her ?"

"I'm not good at fine words, Mabyn. You'll see."

She held out her hand to him, and pressed his warmly.

"I believe you will be a good husband to her; and I know you will get the best wife in the whole world !"

She was going away when he suddenly said—

"Mabyn !"

She turned.

"Do you know," said he rather shame-facedly, "how much I am grateful to you for all your frank straightforward kindness—and your help—and your courage——"

"No, no!" said the young girl, good-humouredly. "You make Wenna happy, and don't consider me!"

CHAPTER VII.

UNDER THE WHITE STARS.

DURING the whole glad evening Wenna had been Queen of the Feast, and her subjects had obeyed her with a joyous submission. They did not take quite so kindly to Mabyn, for she was sharp of tongue and imperious in her ways; but they knew that they could tease her elder sister with impunity— always up to the well-understood line at which her authority began. That was never questioned.

Then, at nine o'clock, the servants came, some on foot and some on dog-carts; and presently there was a bundling up of tiny figures in rugs and wraps and Wenna stood at the door to kiss each of them and say good-bye. It was half-past nine when that performance was over.

"Now, my dear Miss Wenna," said the old clergyman, "you must be quite tired out with your labours. Come into the study—I believe the tray has been taken in there."

"Do you know, Mr. Trewhella," said Mabyn boldly, "that Wenna hadn't time to eat a single bit when all those children were gobbling up cake. Couldn't you let her have a little bit—a little bit of cold meat now——"

"Dear, dear me!" said the kind old gentleman, in the deepest distress, "that I should not have remembered!"

There was no use in Wenna protesting. In the snug little study she was made to eat some supper; and if she got off with drinking one glass of sherry it was not through the intervention of her sister, who apparently would have had her drink a tumbler-full.

It was not until a quarter past ten that the girls could get away.

"Now I must see you young ladies down to the village, lest some one should run away with you," the old clergyman said, taking down his top coat.

"Oh no, you must not—you must not, indeed, Mr. Trewhella!" Mabyn said, anxiously. "Wenna and I always go about by ourselves—and far later than this too. It is a beautiful, clear night! Why——"

Her impetuosity made her sister smile.

"You talk as if you would rather like to be run away with, Mabyn," she said. "But indeed, Mr. Trewhella, you must not think of coming with us. It is quite true what Mabyn says."

And so they went out into the clear darkness together; and the door was shut; and they found themselves in the silent

world of the night-time, with the white
stars throbbing overhead. Far away in the
distance they could hear the murmur of the
sea.

"Are you cold, Mabyn, that you
tremble so ?" said the elder sister.

"No—only a sort of shiver in coming
out into the night air."

Whatever it was it was soon over.
Mabyn seemed to be unusually cheerful.

"Wenna," she said, "you're afraid of
ghosts ! "

"No, I'm not."

"I know you are."

"I'm not half as much afraid of ghosts
as you are, that's quite certain."

"I'll bet you you won't walk down
through the wood."

"Just now ?"

"Yes."

"Why, I'll not only go down through
the wood, but I'll undertake to be home

before you, though you've a broad road to guide you."

"But I did not mean you to go alone."

"Oh," said Wenna, "you propose to come with me? Then it is you who are afraid to go down by yourself? Oh, Mabyn!"

"Never mind, Wenna,—let's go down through the wood just for fun."

So the two sisters set out, arm-in-arm; and through some spirit of mischief Wenna would not speak a word. Mabyn was gradually overawed by the silence, the night, the loneliness of the road, and the solemn presence of the great living vault above them. Moreover, before getting into the wood, they had to skirt a curious little dingle, in the hollow of which are both a church and churchyard. Many a time the sisters had come up to this romantic dell in the spring-time, to gather splendid prim-roses, sweet violets, the yellow celandine,

and other wild flowers that grow luxu-
riantly on its steep banks; and very pretty
the old church looked then, with the clear
sunshine of April streaming down through
the scantily-leaved trees into this seques-
tered spot. Now the deep hole was black
as night; and they could only make out a
bit of the spire of the church as it appeared
against the dark sky. Nay, was there not a
sound among the fallen leaves and under-
wood down there, in the direction of the
unseen graves?

"Some cow has strayed in there, I
believe," said Mabyn, in a somewhat low
voice, and she walked rather quickly until
they got past the place and out on to the
hill over the wooded valley.

"Now," said Wenna, cheerfully, not
wishing to have Mabyn put in a real fright,
"as we go down I am going to tell you
something, Mabyn. How would you like to
have to prepare for a wedding in a fortnight?"

"Not at all!" said Mabyn promptly, even fiercely.

"Not if it was your own?"

"No—why, the insult of such a request!"

According to Mabyn's way of thinking it was an insult to ask a girl to marry you in a fortnight, but none to insist on her marrying you the day after to-morrow.

"You think that a girl could fairly plead that as an excuse—the mere time to get one's dresses and things ready?"

"Certainly!"

"Oh, Mabyn," said Wenna, far more seriously, "it is not of dresses I am thinking at all; but I shudder to think of getting married just now. I could not do it. I have not had enough time to forget what is past—and until that is done, how could I marry any man?"

"Wenna, I do love you when you talk like that!" her sister cried. "You can be so wise and reasonable when you choose! Of course you are quite right, dear. But you don't mean to say he wants you to get married before he goes to Jamaica, and then to leave you alone?"

"Oh, no. He wants me to go with him to Jamaica."

Mabyn uttered a short cry of alarm.

"To Jamaica! To take you away from the whole of us—why—oh, Wenna, I do hate being a girl so—for you're not allowed to swear—if I were a man now! To Jamaica! Why don't you know that there are hundreds of people always being killed there by the most frightful hurricanes, and earthquakes, and large serpents in the woods? To Jamaica?—no, you are not going to Jamaica just yet! I don't think you are going to Jamaica just yet!"

"No, indeed, I am not," said Wenna, with a quiet decision. "Nor could I think of getting married in any case at present.

But then—don't you see, Mabyn—Mr. Roscorla is just a little peculiar in some ways——

"Yes, certainly!"

"——and he likes to have a definite reason for what you do. If I were to tell him of the repugnance I have to the notion of getting married just now, he would call it mere sentiment, and try to argue me out of it—then we should have a quarrel. But if, as you say, a girl may fairly refuse in point of time——"

"Now, I'll tell you," said Mabyn, plainly; "no girl can get married properly, who hasn't six months to get ready in. She might manage in three or four months, for a man she was particularly fond of; but if it is a mere stranger—and a disagreeable person—and one who ought not to marry her at all—then six months is the very shortest time. Just you send Mr. Roscorla to me, and I'll tell him all about it."

Wenna laughed.

"Yes, I've no doubt you would. I think he's more afraid of you than of all the serpents and snakes in Jamaica."

"Yes, and he'll have more cause to be before he's much older," said Mabyr, confidently.

They could not continue their conversation just then, for they were going down the side of the hill, between short trees and bushes; and the path was broad enough only for one, while there were many dark places demanding caution.

"Seen any ghosts yet?" Wenna called out to Mabyn, who was behind her.

"Ghosts, sir? Ay, ay, sir! Heave away on the larboard beam! I say, Wenna, isn't it uncommon dark?"

"It is uncommonly dark."

"Gentlemen always say uncommon; and all the grammars are written by gentlemen. Oh, Wenna, wait a bit; I've lost my brooch!"

It was no *ruse*, for a wonder; the brooch had, indeed, dropped out of her shawl. She felt all over the dark ground for it, but her search was in vain.

"Well, here's a nice thing! Upon my——"

"Mabyn!"

"Upon my —— trotting pony; that was all I was going to say. Wenna, will you stay here for a minute; and I'll run down to the foot of the hill, and get a match?"

"How can you get a match at the foot of the hill? You'll have to go on to the inn. No, tie your handkerchief round the foot of one of the trees, and come up early in the morning to look."

"Early in the morning?" said Mabyn. "I hope to be in——I mean asleep then."

Twice she had nearly blurted out the secret; and, it is highly probably that her refusal to adopt Wenna's suggestion would have led her sister to suspect something, had not Wenna herself, by accident, kicked against the missing brooch. As it was, the time lost by this misadventure was grievous to Mabyn, who now insisted on leading the way, and went along through the bushes at a rattling pace. Here and there the belated wanderers startled a blackbird, that went shrieking its fright over to the other side of the valley; but Mabyn was now too much pre-occupied to be unnerved.

"Keeping a look out a-head?" Wenna called.

"Ay, ay, sir! No ghosts on the weather quarter! Ship drawing twenty fathoms, and the mate fast asleep. Oh, Wenna, my hat!"

It had been twitched off her head by one of the branches of the young trees through which she was passing, and the pliant bit of wood, being released from the strain, had thrown it down into the dark bushes and briars.

"Well I'm—no, I'm not!" said Mabyn, as she picked out the hat from among the thorns, and straightened the twisted feather. Then she set out again, impatient over these delays; and yet determined not to let her courage sink.

"Land ahead yet?" called out Wenna.

"Ay, ay, sir; and the Lizard on our lea! Wind S.S.W., and the cargo shifting a point to the east. Hurrah!"

"Mabyn, they'll hear you a mile off!"

It was certainly Mabyn's intention that she should be heard at least a quarter of a mile off, for now they had got down to the open, and they could hear the stream some way ahead of them, which they would have to cross. At this point Mabyn paused for a second to let her sister overtake her; then they went on arm-in-arm.

·"Oh, Wenna," she said, "do you remember '*young Lochinvar*'?"

"Of course!"

"Didn't you fall in love with him when you read about him ? Now, there *was* somebody to fall in love with! Don't you remember when he came into Netherby Hall, that

The bride-maidens whispered, ' 'Twere better by far
To have matched our fair cousin with young Lochinvar!'

And then you know, Wenna—

One touch to her hand, and one word in her ear,
When they reached the hall-door, and the charger stood near;
So light to the croupe the fair lady he swung,
So light to the saddle before her he sprung!
' She is won! we are gone—over bank, bush, and scaur!
They'll have fleet steeds that follow,' quoth young Lochinvar.

That *was* a lover now!"

"I think he was a most impertinent young man," said Wenna.

"I rather like a young man to be impertinent," said Mabyn, boldly.

"Then there won't be any difficulty about fitting you with a husband," said Wenna with a light laugh.

Here Mabyn once more went on ahead, picking her steps through the damp grass.

as she made her way down to the stream. Wenna was still in the highest of spirits.

"Walking the plank yet, boatswain?" she called out.

"Not yet, sir," Mabyn called in return. "Ship wearing round on the leeward tack, and the waves running mountains high. Don't you hear 'em, captain?"

"Look out for the breakers, boatswain!"

"Ay, ay, sir. All hands on deck to man the captain's gig! Belay away there! Avast! Mind, Wenna; here's the bridge!"

Crossing over that single plank, in the dead of the night, was a sufficiently dangerous experiment; but both these young ladies had had plenty of experience in keeping their wits about them in more perilous places.

"Why are you in such a hurry, Mabyn?" Wenna said, when they had crossed.

Mabyn did not know what to answer, she was very much excited; and inclined to

talk at random merely to cover her anxiety.
She was now very late for the appointment,
and who could tell what unfortunate misadventure Harry Trelyon might have met
with?

" Oh, I don't know," she said. ' Why
don't you admire young Lochinvar?
Wenna, you're like the Lacedæmons."

" Like the what?"

" Like the Lacedæmons, that were
neither cold nor hot. Why don't you
admire young Lochinvar?"

" Because he was interfering with another man's property."

" That man had no right to her," said
Mabyn, talking rather wildly, and looking
on ahead, to the point at which the path
through the meadows went up the road,
" he was a wretched animal, I know; I
believe he was a sugar broker, and had just
come home from Jamaica."

" I believe," said Wenna, " I believe
that young Lochinvar——"

She stopped.

"What's that!" she said. "What are those two lights up there?"

"They're not ghosts: come along, Wenna!" said Mabyn, hurriedly.

Let us go up to this road, where Harry Trelyon, tortured with anxiety and impatience, is waiting. He had slipped away from the house, pretty nearly as soon as the gentlemen had gone into the drawing-room after dinner; and on some excuse or other had got the horses put to a light and yet roomy Stanhope phaeton. From the stable-yard he drove by a back way into the main road without passing in front of the Hall; then he quietly walked the horses down the steep hill, and round the foot of the valley to the point at which Mabyn was to make her appearance.

But he dared not stop there; for now and again some passer-by came along the

road; and even in the darkness Mrs. Trelyon's grey horses would be recognised by
any of the inhabitants of Eglosilyan, who
would naturally wonder what Master Harry
was waiting for. He walked them a few
hundred yards one way, then a few hundred
yards the other; and ever, as it seemed to
him, the danger was growing greater of
some one from the inn or from the Hall
suddenly appearing and spoiling the whole
plan.

Half-past ten arrived; and nothing could
be heard of the girls. Then a horrible
thought struck him that Roscorla might
by this time have left the Hall; and would
he not be coming down to this very road
on his way up to Basset Cottage? This
was no idle fear; it was almost a matter
of certainty.

The minutes rolled themselves out into
ages; he kept looking at his watch every few
seconds; yet he could hear nothing from

the wood or the valley of Mabyn's approach. Then he got down into the road, walked a few yards this way and that apparently to stamp the nervousness out of his system, patted the horses, and, finally, occupied himself in lighting the lamps. He was driven by the delay into a sort of desperation. Even if Wenna and Mabyn did appear now, and if he was successful in his prayer, there was every chance of their being interrupted by Roscorla, who had without doubt left the Hall some time before.

Suddenly he stopped in his excited walking up and down. Was that a faint 'Hurrah!' that he heard in the distance? He went down to the stile at the junction of the path and the road; and listened attentively. Yes, he could hear at least one voice, as yet a long way off; but now he had no more doubt. He walked quickly back to the carriage.

"Ho, ho, my hearties!" he said, stroking the heads of the horses, "you'll have a Dick Turpin's ride to night."

All the nervousness had gone from him now; he was full of a strange sort of exultation—the joy of a man who feels that the crisis in his life has come, and that he has the power and courage to face it.

He heard them come up through the meadow to the stile; it was Wenna who was talking; Mabyn was quite silent. They came along the road.

"What is this carriage doing here?" Wenna said.

They drew still nearer.

"They are Mrs. Trelyon's horses—and there is no driver——"

At this moment Harry Trelyon came quickly forward and stood in the road before her; while Mabyn as quickly went on and disappeared. The girl was startled, bewildered, but not frightened; for in a

second he had taken her by the hand, and
then she heard him say to her, in an
anxious, low, imploring voice :—

"Wenna, my darling, don't be alarmed!
See here, I have got everything ready to
take you away—and Mabyn is coming with
us—and you know I love you so that I
can't bear the notion of your falling into
that man's hands. Now, Wenna, don't
think about it! Come with me! We shall
be married in London—Mabyn is coming
with you——"

For one brief second or two she seemed
stunned and alarmed; then, looking at
the carriage, and the earnest suppliant before her, the whole truth appeared to flash
in upon her. She looked wildly round.

"Mabyn——" she was about to say,
when he guessed the meaning of her rapid
look.

"Mabyn is here. She is quite close by
—she is coming with us. My darling,

won't you let me save you! This indeed is
our last chance. Wenna!——"

She was trembling so that he thought
she would fall; and he would have put his
arms round her, but that she drew back,
and in so doing, she got into the light, and
then he saw the immeasurable pity and sadness of her eyes.

"Oh, my love," she said, with the tears
running down her face, "I love you! I
will tell you that now, when we speak for
the last time. See, I will kiss you—and
then you will go away——"

"I will not go away—not without you—
this night. Wenna, dearest, you have let
your heart speak at last—now let it tell you
what to do!"

"Oh, must I go? Must I go?" she
said; and then she looked wildly round
again.

"Mabyn!" called out Trelyon, half
mad with joy and triumph, "Mabyn, come

along! Look sharp, jump in! This way,
my darling!"

And he took the trembling girl, and half
lifted her into the carriage.

"Oh, my love, what am I doing for you
this night!" she said to him, with her eyes
swimming in tears.

But what was the matter with Mabyn?
She was just putting her foot on the iron
step when a rapidly approaching figure
caused her to utter a cry of alarm, and she
stumbled back into the road again. The
very accident that Trelyon had been antici-
pating had occurred; here was Mr. Roscorla, bewildered at first, and then blind
with rage when he saw what was happening
before his eyes. In his desperation and
anger he was about to lay hold of Mabyn by
the arm when he was sent staggering back-
wards half-a-dozen yards.

"Don't interfere with me now, or by
God I will kill you!" Trelyon said, be-

tween his teeth ; and then he hurried Mabyn into the carriage.

What was the sound then that the still woods heard, under the throbbing stars, through the darkness that lay over the land ? Only the sound of horses' feet, monotonous and regular, and not a word of joy or sorrow uttered by any one of the party thus hurrying on through the night.

CHAPTER VIII.

INTO CAPTIVITY.

Towards eleven o'clock that night, Mrs. Rosewarne became a little anxious about her girls, and asked her husband to go and meet them, or to fetch them away if they were still at Mr. Trewhella's house.

"Can't they look after themselves?" said George Rosewarne. "I'll be bound Mabyn can any way. Let her alone to come back when she pleases."

Then his wife began to fret; and, as this made him uncomfortable, he said he would walk up the road and meet them. He had no intention of doing so, of course; but it was a good excuse for getting away from a fidgety wife. He went outside into the clear starlight, and lounged down to the small bridge beside the mill, contentedly smoking his pipe.

There he encountered a farmer who was riding home a cob he had bought that day at Launceston; and the farmer and he began to have a chat about horses suggested by that circumstance. Oddly enough, their random talk came round to young Trelyon.

"Your thoroughbreds won't do for this county," George Rosewarne was saying, "to go flying a stone wall and breaking your neck. No, sir! I'll tell you what sort of hunter I should like to have for these parts. I'd have him half-bred, short in the leg, short in the pastern, short in the back, a good sloping shoulder, broad in the chest and the forehead, long in the belly, and just the least bit over fifteen hands—eh! Mr. Thoms? I don't think beauty's of much consequence when your neck's in question. Let him be as angular and ragged in the hips as you like, so long's his ribs are well up to the hip-bone. Have you seen that black horse that young Trelyon rides?"

"'Tis a noble beast, sir—a noble beast," the farmer said; and he would probably have gone on to state what ideal animal had been constructed by his lavish imagination had not a man come running up at this moment, breathless and almost speechless.

"Rosewarne," stammered Mr. Roscorla, "a—a word with you! I want to say——"

The farmer, seeing he was in the way, called out a careless good-night, and rode on.

"Well, what's the matter?" said George Rosewarne a little snappishly: he did not like being worried by excitable people.

"Your daughters!" gasped Mr. Roscorla. "They've both run away—both of them—this minute—with Trelyon! You'll have to ride after them. They're straight away along the high road."

"Both of them? the infernal young fools!" said Rosewarne. "Why the devil didn't you stop them yourself?"

"How could I?" Roscorla said, amazed that the father took the flight of his daughters with apparent equanimity. "You must make haste, Mr. Rosewarne, or you'll never catch them."

"I've a good mind to let 'em go," said he sulkily, as he walked over to the stables of the inn. "The notion of a man having to set out on a wild-goose chase at this time o' night! Run away, have they; and what in all the world have they run away for?"

It occurred to him, however, that the sooner he got a horse saddled and set out, the less distance he would have to go in pursuit; and that consideration quickened his movements.

"What's it all about?" said he to Ros-corla, who had followed him into the stable.

"I suppose they mean a runaway match," said Mr. Roscorla, helping to saddle George Rosewarne's cob, a famous trotter.

"It's that young devil's limb, Mabyn, I'll be bound," said the father. "I wish to heaven somebody would marry her—I don't care who. She's always up to some confounded mischief."

"No, no, no!" Roscorla said; "it's Wenna he means to marry."

"Why, you were to have married Wenna——"

"Yes, but——"

"Then why didn't you? So she's run away, has she?"

George Rosewarne grinned: he saw how the matter lay.

"This is Mabyn's work, I know," said he, as he put his foot in the stirrup, and sprang into the saddle. "You'd better go home, Roscorla. Don't you say a word to anybody. You don't want the girl made a fool of all through the place."

So George Rosewarne set out to bring back his daughters; not galloping as an anxious parent might, but going ahead with a long, steady-going trot, which he knew would soon tell on Mrs. Trelyon's over-fed and under-exercised horses.

"If they mean Plymouth," he was thinking, "as is most likely from their taking the high road, he'll give it them gently at first. And so that young man wants to marry our Wenna. Twould be a fine match for her; and yet she's worth all the money he's got—she's worth it every farthing. I'd give him the other one cheap enough."

Pounding along a dark road, with the consciousness that the further you go the further you've got to get back, and that the distance still to be done is an indeterminate quantity, is agreeable to no one; but it was especially vexatious to George Rosewarne, who liked to take things quietly, and could not understand what all the fuss was about. Why should he be sent on this mad chase at midnight? If anybody wanted to marry either of the girls, why didn't he do so, and say no more about it? Rosewarne had been merely impatient and annoyed when he set out; but the longer he rode, and the more he communed with himself, the deeper grew his sense of the personal injury that had been done him by this act of folly.

It was a very lonely ride indeed. There was not a human being abroad at that hour. When he passed a few cottages from time to time, the windows were dark. Then they had just been putting down a lot of loose stones at several parts of the road, which caused Mr. Rosewarne to swear.

"I'll bet a sovereign," said he to himself, "that old Job kept them a quarter of an hour before he opened Paddock's Gate. I believe the old fool goes to bed. Well, they've waked him up for me any way."

There was some consolation in this surmise, which was well founded. When Rosewarne reached the toll-bar, there was at least a light in the small house. He struck on the door with the handle of his riding-whip, and called out—

"Hi, hi! Job! Come out, you old fool!"

An old man, with very bandy legs, came hobbling out of the toll-house, and went to open the gate, talking and muttering to himself—

"Ay, ay! so yü be agwoin' after the young uns, Maister Rosewarne? Ay, ay! yü'll go up many a lane, and by many a fuzzy 'ill, and acrass a bridge or two afore yü come up wi' 'en, Maister Rosewarne."

"Look sharp, Job!" said Rosewarne. "Carriage been through here lately?"

"Ay, ay, Maister Rosewarne! 'tis a good half-hour agone."

"A half-hour, you idiot?" said Rosewarne, now in a thoroughly bad temper. "You've been asleep and dreaming. Here, take your confounded money!"

So he rode on again, not believing, of course, old Job's malicious fabrication, but being rendered all the same a little uncomfortable by it. Fortunately, the cob had not been out before that day.

More deep lanes, more high, open, windy spaces, more silent cottages, more rough stones; and always the measured fall of the cob's feet and the continued shining and throbbing of the stars overhead. At last, far away ahead, on the top of a high incline, he caught sight of a solitary point of ruddy fire, which presently disappeared. That, he concluded, was the carriage he was pursuing going round a corner, and showing only the one lamp as it turned. They were not so far in front of him as he had supposed.

But how to overtake them? So soon as they heard the sound of his horse would they dash onward at all risks, and have a race for it all through the night? In that case, George Rosewarne inwardly resolved that they might go to Plymouth, or into the deep sea beyond, before he would injure his favourite cob.

On the other hand, he could not bring them to a standstill by threatening to shoot at his own daughters, even if he had had anything with him that would look like a pistol. Should he have to rely then on the moral terrors of a parent's authority? George Rosewarne was inclined to laugh when he thought of his overawing in this fashion the high spirit of his younger daughter.

By slow and sure degrees he gained on

the fugitives; and as he could now catch some sound of the rattling of the carriage-wheels, they must also hear his horse's footfall. Were they trying to get away from him? On the contrary, the carriage stopped altogether.

That was Harry Trelyon's decision. For some time back he had been listening attentively. At length he said—

"Don't you hear some one riding back there?"

"Yes, I do!" said Wenna, beginning to tremble.

"I suppose it is Mr. Roscorla coming after us," the young man said coolly. "Now I think it would be a shame to drag the old gentlemen halfway down to Plymouth. He must have had a good spell already. Shall I stop, and persuade him to go back home to bed?"

"Oh, no!" said Mabyn, who was all for getting on at any risk.

"Oh, no!" Wenna said, fearing the result of an encounter between the two men.

"I must stop," Trelyon said. "It's such precious hard lines on him. I shall easily persuade him that he would be better at home."

So he pulled up the horses, and quietly waited by the roadside for a few minutes. The unknown rider drew nearer and more near.

"That isn't Roscorla's pony," said Trelyon, listening. "That's more like your father's cob."

"My father!" said Wenna in a low voice.

"My darling, you needn't be afraid, whoever it is," Trelyon said.

"Certainly not," added Mabyn, who was far more uncomfortable than she chose to appear. "Who can prevent us going on? They don't lock you up in convents now-a-days. If it is Mr. Roscorla, you just let me talk to him."

Their doubt on that head was soon set at rest. White Charley, with his long swinging trot, soon brought George Rose-warne up to the side of the phaeton, and the girls, long ere he had arrived, had recognised in the gloom the tall figure of their father. Even Mabyn was a trifle nervous.

But George Rosewarne—perhaps because he was a little pacified by their having stopped—did not rage and fume as a father is expected to do whose daughter has run away from him. As soon as he had pulled up his horse, he called out in a petulant tone—

" Well ! what the devil is all this about ? "

" I'll tell you, sir," said Trelyon, quite respectfully and quite firmly. " I wished to marry your daughter Wenna——"

"And why couldn't you do that in Eglo-silyan, instead of making a fool of everybody all around?" Rosewarne said, still talking in an angry and vexed way, as of one who had been personally injured.

"Oh, dada!" Mabyn cried, "you don't know how it happened; but they couldn't have got married there. There's that horrid old wretch, Mr. Roscorla — and Wenna was quite a slave to him, and afraid of him—and the only way was to carry her away from him—and so——"

"Hold your tongue, Mabyn!" her father said. "You'd drive a windmill with your talk!"

"But what she says is true enough," Trelyon said. "Roscorla has a claim on her—this was my only chance, and I took it. Now look here, Mr. Rosewarne; you've a right to be angry and all that—perhaps you are; but what good will it do you to see Wenna left to marry Roscorla?"

"What good will it do me?" said George Rosewarne pettishly. "I don't care which of you she marries——"

"Then you'll let us go on, dada?" Mabyn cried. "Will you come with us? Oh, do come with us! We're only going to Plymouth."

Even the angry father could not withstand the absurdity of this appeal. He burst into a roar of ill-tempered laughter.

"I like that!" he cried. "Asking a man to help his daughter to run away from his own house! It's my impression, my young mistress, that you're at the bottom of all this nonsense. Come, come! enough of it, Trelyon! be a sensible fellow, and turn your horses round—why, the notion of going to Plymouth at this time o' night!"

Trelyon looked at his companion. She put her hand on his arm, and said, in a trembling whisper—

"Oh, yes! pray let us go back."

" You know what you are going to, then ? " said he coldly.

She trembled still more.

" Come, come ! " said her father, " you mustn't stop here all night. You may thank me for preventing your becoming the talk of the whole country."

" I shouldn't have minded that much," Mabyn said ruefully, and very like to cry, indeed, as the horses set out upon their journey back to Eglosilyan.

It was not a pleasant journey for any of them—least of all for Wenna Rosewarne, who, having been bewildered by one wild glimpse of liberty, felt with terror and infinite sadness and despair the old manacles closing round her life again. And what although the neighbours might remain in ignorance of what she had done ? She herself knew, and that was enough.

" You think no one will know ? " Mabyn called out spitefully to her father. " Do you think old Job at the gate has lost either his tongue or his nasty temper?"

"Leave Job to me," the father replied.

When they got to Paddock's Gate the old man had again to be roused, and he came out grumbling.

"Well, you discontented old sinner!" Rosewarne called to him, "don't you like having to earn a living?"

"A fine livin' to wait on folks that don't knaw their own mind, and keep comin' and goin' along the road o' nights like a weaver's shuttle. Hm!"

"Well, Job, you shan't suffer for it this time," Rosewarne said. "I've won my bet. If you made fifty pounds by riding a few miles out, what would you give the gate-keeper?"

Even that suggestion failed to inveigle Job into a better humour.

"Here's a sovereign for you, Job. Now go to bed. Good night!"

How long the distance seemed to be ere they saw the lights of Eglosilyan again! There were only one or two small points of red fire, indeed, where the inn stood. The rest of the village was buried in darkness.

"Oh! what will mother say?" Wenna said in a low voice to her sister.

"She will be very sorry we did not get away altogether," Mabyn answered. "And of course it was Mr. Roscorla who spoiled it. Nobody knew anything about it but himself. He must have run on to the inn and told some one. Wasn't it mean, Wenna? Couldn't he see that he wasn't wanted?"

"Are you talking of Mr. Roscorla?" Trelyon said—George Rosewarne was a bit ahead at this moment. "I wish to goodness I had gagged him and slung him below the phaeton. I knew he would be coming down there. I expected him every moment. Why were you so late, Mabyn?"

"Oh! you needn't blame me, Mr. Trelyon," said Mabyn, rather hurt. " You
know I did everything I could for you."

" I know you did, Mabyn : I wish it had
turned out better."

What was this, then, that Wenna heard,
as she sate there, bewildered, apprehensive,
and sad-hearted ?   Had her own sister
joined in this league to carry her off? It
was not merely the audacity of young
Trelyon that had led to their meeting ?
But she was altogether too frightened and
wretched to be angry.

As they got down into Eglosilyan, and
turned the sharp corner over the bridge,
they did not notice the figure of a man
who had been concealing himself in the
darkness of a shed belonging to a slate-
yard. So soon as they had passed, he went
some little way after them until, from the
bridge, he could see them stop at the door
of the inn. Was it Mrs. Rosewarne who

came out of the glare, and with something like a cry of delight caught her daughter in her arms? He watched the figures go inside, and the phaeton drive away up the hill; then, in the perfect silence of the night, he turned and slowly made his way towards Basset Cottage.

CHAPTER IX.

NEXT morning George Rosewarne was seated on the old oak bench in front of the inn, reading a newspaper. Happening to look up, he saw Mr. Roscorla hurrying towards him over the bridge, with no very pleasant expression on his face. As he came nearer, he saw that the man was strangely excited.

"I want to see your daughter alone," he said.

"You needn't speak as if I had tried to run away with her," Rosewarne answered, with more good nature than was his wont. "Well, go indoors. Ask for her mother."

As Roscorla passed him there was a look in his eyes which rather startled George Rosewarne.

"Is it possible," he asked himself, "that this elderly chap is really badly in love with our Wenna?"

But another thought struck him. He suddenly jumped up, followed Roscorla into the passage, where the latter was standing, and said to him—

"Don't you be too harsh with Wenna. She's only a girl; and they're all alike." This hint, however discourteous in its terms, had some significance as coming from a man who was six inches taller than Mr. Roscorla.

Mr. Roscorla was shown into an empty room. He marched up and down looking at nothing. He was simply in an ungovernable rage.

Wenna came, and shut the door behind her; and for a second or so he stared at her as if expecting her to burst into passionate professions of remorse. On the contrary, there was something more than calmness in her appearance—there was the desperation of a hunted animal that is driven to turn upon its pursuer in the mere agony of helplessness.

"Well!" said he—for, indeed, his passion almost deprived him of his power of speech—"what have you to say? Perhaps nothing? It is nothing, perhaps, to a woman to be treacherous—to tell smooth lies to your face, and to go plotting against you behind your back? You have nothing to say? You have nothing to say?"

"I have nothing to say," she said, with some little sadness in her voice, "that would excuse me, either to you or myself—yes! I know that. But—but I did not intentionally deceive you——"

He turned away with an angry gesture.

"Indeed, indeed I did not," she said

piteously. "I had mistaken my own feelings—the temptation was too great. Oh, Mr. Roscorla! you need not say harsh things of me, for indeed I think worse of myself than you can do."

"And I suppose you want forgiveness now?" he added bitterly. "But I have had enough of that. A woman pledges you her affection, promises to marry you, professes to have no doubts as to the future; and all the while she is secretly encouraging the attentions of a young jackanapes who is playing with her and making a fool of her——"

Wenna Rosewarne's cheeks began to burn red: a less angry man would have taken warning.

"Yes—playing with her and making a fool of her. And for what? To pass an idle time, and make her the bye-word of her neighbours."

"It is not true! it is not true!" she

said indignantly; and there was a dangerous light in her eyes. "If he were here, you would not dare to say such things to me—no, you would not dare!"

"Perhaps you expect him to call after the pretty exploit of last night?" asked Roscorla, with a sneer.

"I do not," she said. "I hope I shall never see him again. It is—it is only misery to every one——"

And here she broke down, in spite of herself. Her anger gave way to a burst of tears.

"But what madness is this?" Roscorla cried. "You wish never to meet him again; yet you are ready at a moment's notice to run away with him, disgracing yourself and your family. You make promises about never seeing him; you break them the instant you get the opportunity. You profess that your girlish fancy for a barber's block of a fellow has been got over; and then, as soon as one's back is turned, you reveal your hypocrisy——"

"Indeed I did not mean to deceive you," she said imploringly. "I did believe that all that was over and gone. I thought it was a foolish fancy——"

"And now?" said he hotly.

"Oh, Mr. Roscorla, you ought to pity me instead of being angry with me. I do love him—I cannot help it. You will not ask me to marry you! See, I will undertake not to marry him—I will undertake never to see him again—if only you will not ask me to keep my promise to you. How can I! How can I?"

"Pity you! and these are the confessions you make!" he exclaimed. "Why, are you not ashamed of yourself to say such things to me? And so you would undertake not to marry him? I know what your undertakings are worth!"

He had struck her hard—his very

hardest indeed; but she would not suffer herself to reply, for she believed she deserved far more punishment than he could inflict. All that she could hope for—all that her whole nature cried out for—was that he should not think her treacherous. She had not intentionally deceived him. She had not planned that effort at escape. But when, in a hurried and pathetic fashion, she endeavoured to explain all this to him, he would not listen. He angrily told her he knew well how women could gloss over such matters. He was no schoolboy to be hoodwinked. It was not as if she had had no warning; her conduct before had been bad enough, when it was possible to overlook it on the score of carelessness, but now it was such as would disgrace any woman who knew her honour was concerned in holding to the word she had spoken.

"And what is he?" he cried, mad with

wrath and jealousy. "An ignorant booby! a ploughboy! a lout who has neither the manners of a gentleman nor the education of a day-labourer——"

"Yes, you may well say such things of him now," said she, with her eyes flashing, "when his back is turned. You would not say so if he were here. But he—yes, if he were here—he would tell you what he thinks of you; for he is a gentleman and not a coward."

Angry as he was, Mr. Roscorla was astounded. The fire in her eyes, the flush in her cheeks, the impetuosity of her voice —were these the patient Wenna of old? But a girl betrays herself sometimes, if she happens to have to defend her lover.

"Oh! it is shameful of you to say such things!" she said. "And you know they are not true. There is not any one I have ever seen who is so manly, and frank, and unselfish as Mr. Trelyon—not any one ;

and if I have seen that—if I have admired too much—well, that is a great misfortune, and I have to suffer for it."

"To suffer?—yes," said he, bitterly. "That is a pretty form of suffering that makes you plan a runaway marriage—a marriage that would bring into your possession the largest estates in the North of Cornwall. A very pretty form of suffering! May I ask when the experiment is to be repeated?"

"You may insult me as you like—I am only a woman," she said.

"Insult you?" he cried, with fresh vehemence. "Is it insult to speak the truth? Yesterday forenoon, when I saw you, you were all smiles and smoothness. When I spoke of our marriage, you made no objection. But all the same you knew that at night——"

"I did not know—I did not know!" she said. "You ought to believe me when

I tell you I knew no more about it than you did. When I met him there at night—it was all so sudden, so unexpected—I scarcely knew what I said; but now—but now I have time to think—Oh, Mr. Roscorla, don't think that I do not regret it! I will do anything you ask me—I will promise what you please—indeed, I will undertake never to see him again as long as I live in this world—only, you won't ask me to keep my promise to you——"

He made no reply to this offer; for a step outside the door caused him to mutter something very like an oath between his teeth. The door was thrown open, Mabyn marched in—a little pale, but very erect.

"Mabyn, leave us alone for a moment or two," said Wenna, turning away so as to hide the tears on her face.

"I will not. I want to speak a word or two to Mr. Roscorla."

"Mabyn, I want you to go away just now."

Mabyn went over to her sister, and took her by the hand.

" Wenna, dear, go away to your own room. You've had quite enough—you are trembling all over. I suppose he'll make me tremble next."

" Really, I think your interference is rather extraordinary, Miss Mabyn," said Mr. Roscorla, striving to contain his rage.

" I beg your pardon," said Mabyn, meekly. " I only want to say a word or two. Wouldn't it be better here than before the servants ? "

With that she led Wenna away. In a minute or two she returned. Mr. Roscorla would rather have been shut up in a den with a hungry tigress.

" I am quite at your service," he said with a bitter irony. " I suppose you have some very important communication to make, considering the way in which you——"

"Interfered? Yes, it is time that I interfered," Mabyn said, still quite calm and a trifle pale. "Mr. Roscorla, to be frank, I don't like you, and perhaps I am not quite fair to you. I am only a young girl, and don't know what the world would say about your relations with Wenna. But Wenna is my sister, and I see she is wretched; and her wretchedness—well, that comes of her engagement to you."

She was standing before him, with her eyes cast down, apparently determined to be very moderate in her speech. But there was a cruel frankness in her words which hurt Mr. Roscorla a good deal more than any tempest of passion into which she might have worked herself.

"Is that all?" said he. "You have not startled me with any revelations."

"I was going to say," continued Mabyn, "that a gentleman who has really a regard for a girl would not insist on her keeping a promise which only rendered her unhappy. I don't see what you are to gain by it. I suppose you—you expect Wenna to marry you? Well, I dare say if you called on her to punish herself that way, she might do it. But what good would that do you? Would you like to have a wife who was in love with another man?"

"You have become quite logical, Miss Mabyn," said he, "and argument suits you better than getting into a rage. And much of what you say is quite true. You *are* a very young girl. You don't know much of what the world would say about anything. But being furnished with these admirable convictions, did it never occur to you that you might not be acting wisely in blundering into an affair of which you know nothing?"

The coldly sarcastic fashion in which he spoke threatened to disturb Mabyn's forced equanimity.

"Know nothing?" she said. "I know everything about it; and I can see that my sister is miserable—that is sufficient reason for my interference. Mr. Roscorla, you won't ask her to marry you!"

Had the proud and passionate Mabyn condescended to make an appeal to her ancient enemy? At least she raised her eyes; and they seemed to plead for mercy.

"Come, come," he said, roughly. "I've had enough of all this sham beseeching. I know what it means. Trelyon is a richer man than I am; she has let her idle girlish notions go dreaming day-dreams; and so I am expected to stand aside. There has been enough of this nonsense. She is not a child; she knows what she undertook of her own free will; and she knows she can get rid of this school-girl fancy directly if she chooses. I for one won't help her to disgrace herself."

Mabyn began to breathe a little more

quickly. She had tried to be reasonable; she had even humbled herself and begged from him; now there was a sensation in her chest as of some rising emotion that demanded expression in quick words.

"You will try to make her marry you?" said she, looking him in the face.

"I will try to do nothing of the sort," said he. "She can do as she likes. But she knows what an honourable woman would do."

"And I," said Mabyn, her temper at length quite getting the better of her, "I know what an honourable man would do. He would refuse to bind a girl to a promise which she fears. He would consider her happiness to be of more importance than his comfort. Why, I don't believe you care at all whether Wenna marries you or not— it is only you can't bear her being married to the man she really does love—it is only envy, that's what it is. Oh! I am ashamed to think there is a man alive who would force a girl into becoming his wife on such terms—"

" There is certainly one considerable objection to my marrying your sister," said he, with great politeness. " The manners of some of her relatives might prove embarrassing."

" Yes, that is true enough," Mabyn said, with hot cheeks. " If ever I became a relative of yours, my manners no doubt would embarrass you very considerably. But I am not a relative of yours as yet, nor is my sister."

" May I consider that you have said what you had to say?" said he, taking up his hat.

Proud and angry, and at the same time mortified by her defeat, Mabyn found herself speechless. He did not offer to shake hands with her. He bowed to her in passing out. She made the least possible acknowledgment, and then she was alone. Of course, a hearty cry followed. She felt she had done no good. She had determined to be calm; whereas all the calmness had been on his side, and she had been led into speaking in a manner which a discreet and well-bred young lady would have shrunk from in horror. Mabyn sat still and sobbed, partly in anger and partly in disappointment; she dared not even go to tell her sister.

But Mr. Roscorla, as he went over the bridge again, and went up to Basset Cottage, had lost all his assumed coolness of judgment and demeanour. He felt he had been tricked by Wenna and insulted by Mabyn, while his rival had established a hold which it would be in vain for him to seek to remove. He was in a passion of rage. He would not go near Wenna again. He would at once set off for London and enjoy himself there while his holiday lasted;

he would not write a word to her; then, when the time arrived, he would set sail for Jamaica, leaving her to her own conscience. He was suffering a good deal from anger, envy, and jealousy; but he was consoled by the thought that she was suffering more. And he reflected, with some comfort to himself, that she would scarcely so far demean herself as to marry Harry Trelyon, so long as she knew in her heart what he, Roscorla, would think of her for so doing.

CHAPTER X.

"Has he gone?" Wenna asked of her sister, the next day.

"Yes, he has," Mabyn answered, with a proud and revengeful face. "It was quite true what Mrs. Cornish told me—I've no doubt she had her instructions. He has just driven away to Launceston, on his way to London."

"Without a word!"

"Would you like to have had another string of arguments?" Mabyn said, impatiently. "Oh, Wenna, you don't know what mischief all this is doing. You are awake all night; you cry half the day;

what is to be the end of it? You will work yourself into a fever."

"Yes, there must be an end of it," Wenna said, with decision, "not for myself alone, but for others. That is all the reparation I can make now. No girl in all this country has ever acted so badly as I have done—just look at the misery I have caused—but now——"

"There is one who is miserable, because he loves you," Mabyn said.

"Do you think that Mr. Roscorla has no feelings? You are so unjust to him. Well, it does not matter now: all this must come to an end. Mabyn, I should like to see Mr. Trelyon, just for one minute."

"What will you say to him, Wenna?" her sister said, with a sudden fear.

"Something that it is necessary to say to him, and the sooner it is over the better."

Mabyn rather dreaded the result of this

interview; and yet, she reflected to herself, here was an opportunity for Harry Trelyon to try to win some promise from her sister. Better, in any case, that they should meet than that Wenna should simply drive him away into banishment without a word of explanation.

The meeting was easily arranged. On the next morning, long before Wenna's daily round of duties had commenced, the two sisters left the inn, and went over the bridge, and out to the bold promontory of black rock at the mouth of the harbour. There was nobody about. This October morning was more like a summer-day; the air was mild and still; the blue sky without a cloud; the shining sea plashed around the rocks with the soft murmuring noise of a July calm. It was on these rocks, long ago, that Wenna Rosewarne had pledged herself to become the wife of Mr. Roscorla; and at that time life had seemed to her, if

not brilliant and beautiful, at least grateful
and peaceful.   Now all the peace had gone
out of it.

"Oh, my darling!" Trelyon said, as
she advanced alone towards him—for Mabyn
had withdrawn.   "It is so good of you to
come.   Wenna, what has frightened you?"

He had seized both her hands in his;
but she took them away again.   For one
brief second her eyes had met his, and
there was a sort of wistful and despairing
kindliness in them; then she stood before
him, with her face turned away from him,
and her voice low and tremulous.

"I did wish to see you—for once—for
the last time," she said.   "If you had gone
away, you would have carried with you
cruel thoughts of me.   I wish to ask your
forgiveness——"

"My forgiveness?"

"Yes, for all that you may have suffered; and—for all that may trouble you

in the future—not in the future, but for
the little time you will remember what has
taken place here. Mr. Trelyon, I—I did
not know! Indeed, it is all a mystery to
me now—and a great misery——"

Her lips began to quiver; but she con-
trolled herself.

"And surely it will only be for a short
time, if you think of it at all. You are
young—you have all the world before you.
When you go away among other people
and see all the different things that interest
a young man, you will soon forget whatever has happened here."

"And you say that to me," he said,
"and you said the other night that you
loved me. It is nothing, then, for people
who love each other to go away, and be
consoled, and never see each other again?"

Again the lips quivered: he had no idea
of the terrible effort that was needed to
keep this girl calm.

"I did say that——" she said.

"And it was true?" he broke in.

"It was true then—it is true now—that is all the misery of it!" she exclaimed, with tears starting to her eyes.

"And you talk of our being separated for ever!" he cried. "No!—not if I can help it! Mabyn has told me of all your scruples—they are not worth looking at. I tell you you are no more bound to that man than Mabyn is; and that isn't much. If he is such a mean hound as to insist on your marrying him, then I will appeal to your father and mother, and they must prevent him. Or I will go to him myself, and settle the matter in a shorter way——"

"You cannot now," she said; "he has gone away. And what good would that have done? I would never marry any man unless I could do so with a clear and happy conscience; and if you—if you and Mabyn —see nothing in my treatment of *him* that is wrong, then that is very strange; but I cannot acquit myself. No; I hope no woman will ever treat you as I have treated him. Look at his position—an elderly man, with few friends—he has not all the best of his life before him as you have—or the good spirits of youth—and after he had gone away to Jamaica, taking my promise with him—oh! I am ashamed of myself when I think on all that has happened."

"Then you've no right to be," said he, hotly. "It was the most natural thing in the world, and he ought to have known it, that a young girl who has been argued into engaging herself to an old man should consider her being in love with another man as something of rather more importance—of a good deal more importance, I should say. And his suffering? He suffers no more than this lump of rock does. That is not his way of thinking—to be bothered about anything. He may be angry, yes!—and vexed for the moment, as is natural; but if you think he is going about the world with a load of agony on him, then you're quite mistaken. And if he were, what good could you do by making yourself miserable as well? Wenna, do be reasonable, now."

Had not another, on this very spot, prayed her to be reasonable? She had yielded then. Mr. Roscorla's 'arguments were incontrovertible, and she had shrinkingly accepted the conclusion. Now, young Trelyon's representations and pleadings were far less cogent; but how strongly her heart went with them!

"No!" she said, as if she were shaking off the influence of the temper, "I must not listen to you. Yet you don't seem to think that it costs me anything to ask you to bid me good-bye once and for all. It should be less to you than to me. A girl thinks of these things more than a man— she has little else to think of—he goes out into the world and forgets. And you—you will go away, and you will become such a man as all who know you will love to speak of and be proud of; and some day you will come back, and if you like to come down to the inn, then there will be one or two there glad to see you. Mr. Trelyon, don't ask me to tell you why this should be so. I know it to be right; my heart tells me. Now I will say good-bye to you."

"And when I come back to the inn, will you be there?" said he, becoming rather pale. "No; you will be married to a man whom you will hate."

"Indeed no," she said, with her face flushing and her eyes cast down. "How can that be after what has taken place? He could not ask me. All that I begged of him before he went away was this—that he would not ask me to marry him; and if only he would do that, I promised never to see you again—after bidding you good-bye as I do now."

"And is that the arrangement?" said he, rather roughly. "Are we to play at dog in the manger? He is not to marry you himself; but he will not let any other man marry you?"

"Surely he has some right to consideration," she said.

"Well, Wenna," said he, "if you've made up your mind, there's no more to be said. I think you are needlessly cruel——"

"You won't say that, just as we are parting," she said, in a low voice. "Do you think it is nothing to me?"

He looked at her for a moment with a great sadness and compunction in his eyes; then, moved by an uncontrollable impulse, he caught her in his arms, and kissed her on the lips.

"Now," said he, with his face white as death, "tell me that you will never marry any other man as long as you live!"

"Yes, I will say that," she said to him,

in a low voice, and with a face as white as his own.

"Swear it, then!"

"I have said that I will never marry any other man than you," she said, "and that is enough—for me. But as for you—why must you go away thinking of such things? You will see some day what madness it would have been—you will come some day and thank me for having told you so—and then—and then—if anything should be mentioned about what I said just now, you will laugh at the old half-forgotten joke——"

Well, there was no laughing at the joke just then; for the girl burst into tears, and in the midst of that she hastily pressed his hand, and hurried away. He watched her go round the rocks, to the cleft leading down to the harbour. There she was rejoined by her sister; and the two of them went slowly along the path of broken slate,

with the green hill above, the blue water
below, and the fair sunshine all around
them. Many a time he recalled afterwards
—and always with an increasing weight at
his heart—how sombre seemed to him that
bright October day and the picturesque
opening of the coast leading in to Eglosilyan. For it was the last glimpse of
Wenna Rosewarne that he was to have for
many a day; and a sadder picture was
never treasured up in a man's memory.

"Oh, Wenna, what have you said to
him that you tremble so?" Mabyn asked.

"I have bid him good-bye—that is all."

"Not for always?"

"Yes, for always."

"And he is going away again, then?"

"Yes, as a young man should. Why
should he stop here to make himself
wretched over impossible fancies? He will
go out into the world; and he has splendid
health and spirits; and he will forget all
this."

" And you—you are anxious to forget it all too ? "

" Would it not be better ? What good can come of dreaming ? Well, I've plenty of work to do ; that is well."

Mabyn was very much inclined to cry : all her beautiful visions of the future happiness of her sister had been rudely dispelled. All her schemes and machinations had gone for nothing. There only remained to her, in the way of consolation, the fact that Wenna still wore the sapphire ring that Harry Trelyon had sent her.

" And what will his mother think of you ? " said Mabyn, as a last argument, " when she finds you have sent him away altogether—to go into the army, and go abroad, and perhaps die of yellow fever, or be shot by the Sepoys and the Caffres ? "

" She would have hated me if I had married him," said Wenna, simply.

" Oh, Wenna, how dare you say such a

thing!" Mabyn cried. "What do you
mean by it?"

"Would a lady in her position like her
only son to marry the daughter of an
innkeeper?" Wenna asked, rather indifferently : indeed, her thoughts were elsewhere.

"I tell you there's no one in the world
she loves like you—I can see it every time
she comes down for you—and she believes,
and I believe too, that you have changed
Mr. Trelyon's way of talking and his
manner of treating people in such a fashion
as no one would have considered possible.
Do you think she hasn't eyes? He is
scarcely ever impertinent now—when he is
it is always in good-nature, and never in
sulkiness. Look at his kindness to Mr.
Trewhella's granddaughter ; and Mr. Trewhella a clergyman too. Did he ever use
to take his mother out for a drive? No,
never! And of course she knows whom it's

all owing to; and if you would marry Mr. Trelyon, Wenna, I believe she would worship you and think nothing good enough for you——"

"Mabyn, I am going to ask something of you."

"Oh, yes, I know what it is," her sister said. "I am not to speak any more about your marriage with Mr. Trelyon. But I won't give you any such promise, Wenna. I don't consider that that old man has any hold on you."

Wenna said nothing; for at this moment they entered the house. Mabyn went up with her sister to her room; then she stood undecided for a moment; finally she said—

"Wenna, if I've vexed you, I'm very sorry. I won't speak of Mr. Trelyon if you don't wish it. But indeed you don't know how many people are anxious that you should be happy—and you can't expect your own sister not to be as anxious as any one else——"

"Mabyn, you're a good girl," Wenna said, kissing her. But I am rather tired to-day—I think I shall lie down for a little while——"

Mabyn uttered a sharp cry, for her sister had fallen back on a chair, white and insensible. She hastily bathed her forehead with cold water; she chafed her hands; she got hold of some smelling salts. It was only a faint, after all; and Wenna, having come to, said she would lie down on the sofa for a few minutes. Mabyn said nothing to her mother about all this, for it would have driven Mrs. Rosewarne wild with anxiety; but she herself was rather disquieted with Wenna's appearance, and she said to herself, with great bitterness of heart—

"If my sister falls ill, I know who has done that."

CHAPTER XI.

NEW AMBITIONS.

Mr. Roscorla, having had few friends throughout his life, had developed a most methodical habit of communing with himself on all possible subjects, but more particularly, of course, upon his own affairs. He used up his idle hours in defining his position with regard to the people and things around him, and he was never afraid to convince himself of the exact truth. He never tried to cheat himself into the belief that he was more unselfish than might appear; if other people thought so, good and well. He, at least, was not a hypocrite to himself.

Now, he had not been gone above a couple of hours or so from Eglosilyan when he discovered that he was not weighted with terrible woes ; on the contrary, he experienced a feeling of austere satisfaction that he was leaving a good deal of trouble behind him. He had been badly used ; he had been righteously angry. It was right that they who had thus used him badly should be punished. As for him, if his grief did not trouble him much, that was a happy peculiarity of his temperament which did not lessen their offence against him.

Most certainly he was not weighted with woe. He had a pleasant drive in the morning over to Launceston ; he smoked a cigarette or two in the train. When he arrived at Plymouth, he ordered a very nice luncheon at the nearest hotel, and treated himself to a bottle of the best Burgundy the waiter could recommend him. After that he got into a smoking carriage in the London express; he lit a large cigar; he wrapped a thick rug round his legs, and settled himself down in peace for the long journey. Now was an excellent time to find out exactly how his affairs stood.

He was indeed very comfortable. Leaving Eglosilyan had not troubled him. There was something in the knowledge that he was at last free from all those exciting scenes which a quiet middle-aged man, not believing in romance, found trying to his nervous system. This brief holiday in Eglosilyan had been anything but a pleasant one; was he not, on the whole, glad to get away?

Then he recollected that the long-expected meeting with his betrothed had not been so full of delight as he had anticipated. Was there not just a trace of disappointment in the first shock of feeling at their meeting? She was certainly not a handsome woman—such a one as he might have preferred to introduce to his friends about

Kensington, in the event of his going back to live in London.

Then he thought of old General Weekes. He felt a little ashamed of himself for not having had the courage to tell the General and his wife that he meant to marry one of the young ladies who had interested them. Would it not be awkward, too, to have to introduce Wenna Rosewarne to them in her new capacity?

That speculation carried him on to the question of his marriage. There could be no doubt that his betrothed had become a little too fond of the handsomest young man in the neighbourhood. Perhaps that was natural; but at all events she was now very much ashamed of what had happened, and he might trust her to avoid Harry Trelyon in the future. That having been secured, would not her thoughts naturally drift back to the man to whom she had plighted a troth which was still formally binding on her? Time was on his side. She would forget that young man; she would be anxious, as soon as these temporary disturbances of her affections were over, to atone for the past by her conduct in the future. Girls had very strong notions about duty.

Well, he drove to his club, and finding one of the bedrooms free, he engaged it for a week, the longest time possible. He washed, dressed, and went down to dinner. To his great delight, the first man he saw was old Sir Percy himself, who was writing out a very elaborate *menu*, considering that he was ordering dinner for himself only. He and Mr. Roscorla agreed to dine together.

Now, for some years back Mr. Roscorla, in visiting his club, had found himself in a very isolated and uncomfortable position. Long ago he had belonged to the younger set—to those reckless young fellows who were not afraid to eat a hasty

dinner, and then rush off to take a mother
and a couple of daughters to the theatre,
returning at midnight to some anchovy
toast and a glass of Burgundy, followed by
a couple of hours of brandy-and-soda, cigars,
and billiards. But he had drifted away from
that set; indeed, they had disappeared, and
he knew none of their successors. On the
other hand, he had never got into the ways
of the old-fogey set. Those stout old gentlemen who carefully drank nothing but claret
and seltzer, who took a quarter of an hour
to write out their dinner-bill, who spent the
evening in playing whist, kept very much
to themselves. It was into this set that
the old General now introduced him. Mr.
Roscorla had quite the air of a bashful
young man when he made one of a party of
those ancients, who dined at the same table
each evening. He was almost ashamed to
order a pint of champagne for himself—it
savoured so much of youth. He was silent

in the presence of his seniors ; and indeed
they were garrulous enough to cover his
silence. Their talk was mostly of politics
—not the politics of the country, but the
politics of office ; of under-secretaries and
candidates for place. They seemed to look
on the Government of the country as a sort
of mechanical clock, which from time to
time sent out a few small figures, and from
time to time took them in again ; and they
showed an astonishing acquaintance with
the internal and intricate mechanism which
produced these changes. Perhaps it was
because they were so busy in watching for
changes on the face of the clock that they
seemed to forget the swinging onward of
the great world outside, and the solemn
march of the stars.

Most of those old gentlemen had lived
their life—had done their share of heavy
dining and reckless drinking many years
ago—and thus it was they had. come to

drink seltzer and claret. But it appeared that it was their custom, after dinner, to have the table-cover removed, and some port wine placed on the mahogany. Mr. Roscorla, who had felt as yet no ugly sensations about his finger-joints, regarded this ceremony with equanimity; but it was made the subject of some ominous joking on the part of his companions. Then joking led to joking. There were no more politics. Some very funny stories were told. Occasionally one or two names were introduced, as of persons well known in London society, though not of it; and Mr. Roscorla was surprised that he had never heard these names before—you see how one becomes ignorant of the world if one buries oneself down in Cornwall. Mr. Roscorla began to take quite an interest in these celebrated people, in the price of their ponies, and the diamonds they were understood to have worn at a certain very singular ball. He was pleased to hear, too, of the manner in which the aristocracy of England were resuming their ancient patronage of the arts; for he was given to understand that a young earl or baron could scarcely be considered a man of fashion unless he owned a theatre.

On their way up to the card-room, Mr. Roscorla and one of his venerable companions went into the hall to get their cigar-case from their top-coat pocket. This elderly gentleman had been the governor of an island in the Pacific. He had now been resident for many years in England. He was on the directorate of one or two well-known commercial companies; he had spoken at several meetings on the danger of dissociating religion from education in the training of the young; in short, he was a tower of respectibility. On the present occasion he had to pull out a muffler to get at his cigar-case; and with the muffler came a small parcel tied up in tissue-paper.

"Neat, aren't they?" said he, with a senile grin, showing Mr. Roscorla the tips of a pair of pink satin slippers.

"Yes," said Mr. Roscorla; "I suppose they're for your daughter."

They went up to the card-room.

"I expect you'll teach us a lesson, Roscorla," said the old General. "Gad, some of you West-Indian fellows know the difference between a ten and an ace."

"Last time I played cards," Roscorla said, modestly, "I was lucky enough to win 48l."

"Whew! We can't afford that sort of thing on this side of the water—not if you happen to serve Her Majesty any way. Come, let's cut for partners!"

There was but little talking, of course, during the card-playing; at the end of it Mr. Roscorla found he had only lost half-a-sovereign. Then everybody adjourned to a snug little smoking-room, to which only members were admitted. This, to the neophyte, was the pleasantest part of the evening. He seemed to hear of everything that was going on in London—and a good deal more besides. He was behind the scenes of all the commercial, social, political performances which were causing the vulgar crowd to gape. He discovered the true history of the hostility shown by So-and-so to the Premier; he was told the little scandal which caused Her Majesty to refuse to knight a certain gentleman who had claims on the Government; he heard what the Duke really did offer to the game-keeper whose eye he had shot out, and the language used by the keeper on the occasion; and he received such information about the financial affairs of many a company as made him wonder whether the final collapse of the commercial world were at hand. He forgot that he had heard quite similar stories twenty years before. Then they had been told by ingenuous youths full of the importance of the information they had just acquired; now they were told by garrulous old gentlemen, with a cynical laugh which was more amusing than the hot-headed asseveration of the juniors. It was, on the whole, a delightful evening— this first evening of his return to club-life; and then it was so convenient to go upstairs to bed instead of having to walk from the inn of Eglosilyan to Basset Cottage.

Just before leaving, the old General took Roscorla aside, and said to him—

"Monstrous amusing fellows, eh?"

"Very."

"Just a word. Don't you let old Lewis lug you into any of his companies—you understand?"

"There's not much fear of that!" Mr. Roscorla said, with a laugh. "I haven't a brass farthing to invest."

"All you West-Indians say that; how-

ever, so much the better. And there's old
Strafford, too; he's got some infernal india-
rubber patent. Gad, sir, he knows no more
about those commercial fellows than the
man in the moon; and they'll ruin him—
mark my words, they'll ruin him."

Roscorla was quite pleased to be ad-
vised. It made him feel young and ingenuous. After all, the disparity in years
between him and his late companions was
most obvious.

"And when are you coming to dine
with us, eh?" the General said, lighting a
last cigar and getting his hat. "To-morrow
night?—quiet family party, you know; her
ladyship 'll be awfully glad to see you. Is
it a bargain? All right—seven; we're
early folks. I say—you needn't mention I
dined here to-night; to tell you the truth,
I'm supposed to be looking after a company
too, and precious busy about it. Mum's
the word; d'ye see?"

Really this plunge into a new sort of life was quite delightful. When he went down to breakfast next morning, he was charmed with the order and cleanliness of everything around him; the sunlight was shining in at the large windows; there was a bright fire, in front of which he stood and read the paper until his cutlets came. There was no croaking of an old Cornish housekeeper over her bills; no necessity for seeing if the grocer had been correct in his addition. Then there was a slight difference between the cooking here and that which prevailed in Basset Cottage.

In a comfortable frame of mind he leisurely walked down to Cannon Street, and announced himself to his partners. He sat for an hour or so in a snug little parlour, talking over their joint venture, and describing all that had been done. There was, indeed, every ground for hope; and he was pleased to hear them say that they were

especially obliged to him for having gone
out to verify the reports that had been sent
home, and for his personal supervision
while there. They hoped he would draw
on the joint association for a certain sum
which should represent the value of that
supervision.

Now, if Mr. Roscorla had really been
possessed at this moment of the wealth to
which he looked forward, he would not
have taken so much interest in it. He
would have said to himself—

"What is the life I am to lead, now
that I have this money? Having luncheon
at the club; walking in the Park in the
afternoon; dining with a friend in the evening, and playing whist or billiards, with the
cheerless return to a bachelor's chambers
at night? Is that all that my money can
give me?"

But he had not the money. He looked
forward to it; and it seemed to him that it

contained all the possibilities of happiness. Then he would be free. No more station- ary dragging out of existence in that Cornish cottage. He would move about; he would enjoy life. He was still younger than those jovial old fellows who seemed to be happy enough. When he thought of Wenna Rosewarne, it was with the notion that marriage very considerably hampers a man's freedom of action.

If a man were married, could he have a choice of thirty dishes for luncheon? Could he have the first edition of the evening papers brought him almost damp from the press? Then how pleasant it was to be able to smoke a cigar and to write one or two letters at the same time—in a large and well-ventilated room. Mr. Roscorla did not fail to draw on his partners for the sum they had mentioned; he was not short of money, but he might as well gather the first few drops of the coming shower.

He did not go up to walk in the Park, for he knew there would be almost nobody there at that time of the year; but he walked up to Bond Street and bought a pair of dress-boots, after which he returned to the club, and played billiards with one of his companions of the previous evening, until it was time to dress for dinner.

The party at the General's was a sufficiently small one; for you cannot ask any one to dinner at a few hours' notice, except it be a merry and marriageable widow who has been told that she will meet an elderly and marriageable bachelor. This complaisant lady was present; and Mr. Roscorla found himself on his entrance being introduced to a good-looking, buxom dame, who had a healthy, merry, roseate face, very black eyes and hair, and a somewhat gorgeous dress. She was a trifle demure at first, but her amiable shyness soon wore off, and she was most kind to Mr.

Roscorla. He, of course, had to take in
Lady Weekes; but Mrs. Seton-Willoughby
sate opposite him, and, while keeping the
whole table amused with an account of her
adventures in Galway, appeared to address
the narrative principally to the stranger.

"Oh, my dear Lady Weekes," she said,
"I was so glad to get back to Brighton! I
thought I should have forgotten my own
language, and taken to war-paint and
feathers, if I had remained much longer.
And Brighton is so delightful just now—
just comfortably filled, without the November crush having set in. Now, couldn't you
persuade the General to take you down for
a few days? I am going down on Friday;
and you know how dreadful it is for a poor
lone woman to be in an hotel, especially
with a maid who spends all her time in
flirting with the first-floor waiters. Now
won't you, dear? I assure you the ——
Hotel is most charming—such freedom, and

the pleasant parties they make up in the drawing-room; I believe they have a ball two or three nights a week just now——"

"I should have thought you would have found the —— rather quieter," said Mr. Roscorla, naming a good old-fashioned house.

"Rather quieter?" said the widow, raising her eyebrows. "Yes, a good deal quieter! About as quiet as a dissenting chapel. No, no; if one means to have a little pleasure, why go to such a place as that? Now, will you come and prove the truth of what I have told you?"

Mr. Roscorla looked alarmed; and even the solemn Lady Weekes had to conceal a smile.

"Of course I mean you to persuade our friends here to come too," the widow explained. "What a delightful frolic it would be—for a few days, you' know, to break away from London! Now, my dear, what do you say?"

She turned to her hostess. That small and sombre person referred her to the General. The General, on being appealed to, said he thought it would be a capital joke; and would Mr. Roscorla go with them? Mr. Roscorla, not seeing why he should not have a little frolic of this sort just like any one else, said he would. So they agreed to meet at Victoria Station on the following Friday.

"Struck, eh?" said the old General, when the two gentlemen were alone after dinner. "Has she wounded you, eh? Gad, sir, that woman has 8,000*l*. a year in the India Four per Cents. Would you believe it? Would you believe that any man could have been such a fool as to put such a fortune into India Four per Cents? —with mortgages going a-begging at five, and the marine insurance companies paying thirteen! Well, my boy, what do you think of her? She was most uncommonly

attentive to you, that I'll swear—don't
deny it—now, don't deny it. Bless my
soul, you marrying men are so sly there's
no getting at you. Well, what was I
saying? Yes, yes—will she do? 8,000l. a
year, as I'm a living sinner."

Mr. Roscorla was intensely flattered to
have it even supposed that the refusal of
such a fortune was within his power.

"Well," said he, modestly and yet
critically, "she's not quite my style. I'm
rather afraid of three-deckers. But she
seems a very good-natured sort of woman."

"Good-natured! Is that all you say?
I can tell you, in my time, men were nothing so particular when there was 8,000l.
a year going a-begging."

"Well, well," said Mr. Roscorla, with
a smile. "It is a very good joke. When
she marries, she'll marry a younger man
than I am——"

"Don't you be mistaken—don't you be

mistaken!" the old General cried. "You've made an impression—I'll swear you have; and I told her ladyship you would."

"And what did Lady Weekes say?"

"Gad, sir, she said it would be a deuced good thing for both of you."

"She is very kind," said Mr. Roscorla, pleased at the notion of having such a prize within reach, and yet not pleased that Lady Weekes should have fancied this the sort of woman he would care to marry.

They went to Brighton, and a very pleasant time of it they had at the big, noisy hotel. The weather was delightful. Mrs. Seton-Willoughby was excessively fond of riding; forenoon and afternoon they had their excursions, with the pleasant little dinner of the evening to follow. Was not this a charmed land into which the former hermit of Basset Cottage was straying? Of course, he never dreamed for a moment of marrying this widow; that was out of the question. She was just a little too demonstrative—very clever and amusing for half-an-hour or so, but too gigantic a blessing to be taken through life. It was the mere possibility of marrying her, however, which attracted Mr. Roscorla. He honestly believed, judging by her kindness to him, that, if he seriously tried, he could get her to marry him; in other words, that he might become possessed of 8,000*l.* a year. This money, so to speak, was within his reach; and it was only now that he was beginning to see that money could purchase many pleasures even for the middle-aged. He made a great mistake in imagining, down in Cornwall, that he had lived his life; and that he had but to look forward to mild enjoyments, a peaceful wandering onwards to the grave, and the continual study of economy in domestic affairs. He was only now begin-to live.

"And when are you coming back?" said the widow to him, one evening, when they were all talking of his leaving England.

"That I don't know," he said.

"Of course," she said, "you don't mean to remain in the West Indies. I suppose lots of people have to go there for some object or other, but they always come back when it is attained."

"They come back to attain some other object here," said Mr. Roscorla.

"Then we'll soon find you that," the General burst in. "No man lives out of England who can help it. Don't you find in this country enough to satisfy you?"

"Indeed I do," Mr. Roscorla said, "especially within the last few days. I have enjoyed myself enormously. I shall always have a friendly recollection of Brighton."

"Are you going down to Cornwall before you leave?" Sir Percy asked.

" No," said he, slowly.

" That isn't quite so cheerful as Brighton, eh ? "

" Not quite."

He kept his word. He did not go back to Cornwall before leaving England, nor did he send a single line or message to any one there. It was with something of a proud indifference that he set sail, and also with some notion that he was being amply revenged. For the rest, he hated " scenes ; " and he had encountered quite enough of these during his brief visit to Eglosilyan.

CHAPTER XII.

AN OLD LADY'S APOLOGY.

WHEN Wenna heard that Mr. Roscorla had left England without even bidding her good-bye by letter, she accepted the rebuke with submission, and kept her own counsel. She went about her daily duties with an unceasing industry; Mrs. Trelyon was astonished to see how she seemed to find time for everything. The winter was coming on, and the Sewing Club was in full activity; but even apart from the affairs of that enterprise, Wenna Rosewarne seemed to be everywhere throughout the village, to know everything, to be doing everything that prudent help and friendly counsel could do. Mrs. Trelyon grew to love the girl—in her vague, wondering, simple fashion.

So the days, and the weeks, and the months went by; and the course of life ran smoothly and quietly in the remote Cornish village. Apparently there was nothing to indicate the presence of bitter regrets, of crushed hopes, of patient despair; only Mabyn used to watch her sister at times, and she fancied that Wenna's face was growing thinner.

The Christmas festivities came on, and Mrs. Trelyon was pleased to lend her *protégée* a helping hand in decorating the church. One evening she said—

" My dear Miss Wenna, I am going to ask you an impertinent question. Could your family spare you on Christmas evening? Harry is coming down from London; I am sure he would be so pleased to see you."

" Oh, thank you, Mrs. Trelyon," Wenna said, with just a little nervousness. " You are very kind, but indeed I must be at home on Christmas evening."

"Perhaps some other evening while he is here you will be able to come up," said Mrs. Trelyon, in her gentle way. "You know you ought to come and see how your pupil is getting on. He writes me such nice letters now; and I fancy he is working very hard at his studies, though he says nothing about it."

"I am very glad to hear that," Wenna said, in a low voice.

Trelyon did come to the Hall for a few days, but he kept away from the village, and was seen by no one of the Rosewarnes. But on the Christmas morning, Mabyn Rosewarne, being early about, was told that Mrs. Trelyon's groom wished to see her; and going down, she found the man, with a basket before him.

"Please, miss, Mr. Trelyon's compliments, and would you take the flowers out of the cotton wool, and give them to Miss Rosewarne?"

"Oh, won't I!" said Mabyn, opening the basket at once, and carefully getting out a bouquet of camellias, snowdrops, and sweet violets. "Just you wait a minute, Jakes, for I've got a Christmas-box for you."

Mabyn went upstairs as rapidly as was consistent with the safety of the flowers, and burst into her sister's room.

"Oh, Wenna, look at this! Do you know who sent them? Did you ever see anything so lovely?"

For a second the girl seemed almost frightened; then her eyes grew troubled and moist, and she turned her head away. Mabyn put them gently down, and left the room without a word.

The Christmas and the new year passed without any message from Mr. Roscorla; and Mabyn, though she rebelled against the bondage in which her sister was placed, was glad that she was not disturbed by angry letters. About the middle of January, however, a brief note arrived from Jamaica.

"I cannot let such a time go by," Mr. Roscorla wrote, "whatever may be our relations, without sending you a friendly word. I do hope the new year will bring you health and happiness, and that we shall in time forget the angry manner in which we parted, and all the circumstances leading to it."

She wrote as brief a note in reply, at the end of which she hoped he would forgive her for any pain he had suffered through her. Mabyn was rejoiced to find that the correspondence—whether it was or was not meant on his part to be an offer of reconciliation—stopped there.

And again the slow days went by, until the world began to stir with the new springtime—the saddest time of the year to those who live much in the past. Wenna was out and about a great deal, being continually busy; but she no longer took those long walks by herself in which she used to chat to the butterflies, and the young lambs, and the sea-gulls. The fresh western breezes no longer caused her spirits to flow over in careless gaiety; she saw the new flowers springing out of the earth, but it was of another spring-time she was thinking.

One day, later on in the year, Mrs. Trelyon sent down the wagonnette for her, with the request that she would come up to the Hall for a few minutes. Wenna obeyed the summons, imagining that some business connected with the Sewing Club claimed her attention. When she arrived, she found Mrs. Trelyon unable to express the gladness and gratitude that filled her heart; for before her were certain London newspapers, and behold! Harry Trelyon's name was recorded there in certain lists as having scored a sufficient number of marks in the examination to entitle him to a first commission. It was no concern of hers that his name was pretty far down in the list—enough that he had succeeded somehow. And who was the worker of this miracle—who but the shy, sad-eyed girl standing beside her, whose face wore now a happier expression than it had worn for many a day?

"And this is what he says," the proud mother continued, showing Wenna a letter. " 'It isn't much to boast of, for indeed you'll see by the numbers that it was rather a narrow squeak; anyhow, I pulled through. My old tutor is rather a speculative fellow, and he offered to bet me fifty pounds his coaching would carry me through, which I took; so I shall have to pay him that besides his fees. I must say he has earned both; I don't think a more ignorant person than myself ever went to a man to get crammed. I send you two newspapers;

you might drop one at the inn for Miss Rosewarne any time you are passing; or if you could see her and tell her, perhaps that would be better.' "

Wenna was about as pleased and proud as Mrs. Trelyon was.

" I knew he could do it if he tried," she said, quietly.

"And then," the mother went on to say, " when he has once joined, there will be no money wanting to help him to his promotion; and when he comes back to settle down here, he will have some recognised rank and profession such as a man ought to have. Not that he will remain in the army—for, of course, I should not like to part with him; and he might be sent to Africa, or Canada, or the West Indies. *You* know," she added with a smile, " that it is not pleasant to have any one you care for in the West Indies."

When Wenna got home again, she told

Mabyn. Strange to say, Mabyn did not clap her hands for joy, as might have been expected.

"Wenna," said she, "what made him go into the army? Was it to show you that he could pass an examination? or was it because he means to leave England?"

"I don't know," said Wenna, looking down. "I hope he does not mean to leave England." That was all she said.

Harry Trelyon was, however, about to leave England, though not because he had been gazetted to a colonial regiment. He came down to inform his mother that, on the fifteenth of the month, he would sail for Jamaica; and then and there, for the first time, he told her the whole story of his love for Wenna Rosewarne, of his determination to free her somehow from the bonds that bound her, and, failing that, of the revenge he meant to take. Mrs. Trelyon was amazed, angry, and beseeching in turns.

At one moment she protested that it was madness of her son to think of marrying Wenna Rosewarne; at another, she would admit all that he said in praise of her, and would only implore him not to leave England; or again she would hint that she would almost herself go down to Wenna and beg her to marry him if only he gave up this wild intention of his. He had never seen his mother so agitated; but he reasoned gently with her, and remained firm to his purpose. Was there half as much danger in taking a fortnight's trip in a mail-steamer as in going from Southampton to Malta in a yacht, which he had twice done with her consent?

"Why, if I had been ordered to join a regiment in China, you might have some reason to complain," he said. "And I shall be as anxious as you, mother, to get back again, for I mean to get up my drill thoroughly as soon as I am attached. I have plenty of work before me."

" You're not looking well, Harry," said the mother.

" Of course not," said he, cheerfully. " You don't catch one of those geese at Strasburg looking specially lively when they tie it by the leg and cram it—and that's what I've been going through of late. But what better cure can there be than a sea-voyage ? "

And so it came about that, on a pleasant evening in October, Mr. Roscorla received a visit. He saw the young man come riding up the acacia path, and he instantaneously guessed his mission. His own resolve was taken as quickly.

" Bless my soul, is it you, Trelyon ? " he cried, with apparent delight. " You mayn't believe it, but I am really glad to see you. I have been going to write to you for many a day back. I'll send somebody for your horse ; come into the house."

The young man, having fastened up the bridle, followed his host. There was a calm and business-like rather than a holiday look on his face.

"And what were you going to write to me about?" he asked.

"Oh, you know," said Roscorla, good-naturedly. "You see, a man takes very different views of life when he knocks about a bit. For my part, I am more interested in my business now than in anything else of a more tender character; and I may say that I hope to pay you back a part of the money you lent me as soon as our accounts for this year are made up. Well, about that other point—I don't see how I could well return to England, to live permanently there, for a year or two at the soonest; and—and, in fact—I have often wondered, now, whether it wouldn't be better if I asked Miss Rosewarne to consider herself finally free from that—from that engagement——"

" Yes, I think it would be a great deal better," said Trelyon, coldly. "And perhaps you would kindly put your resolve into writing. I shall take it back to Miss Rosewarne. Will you kindly do so now ? "

" Why ! " said Roscorla, rather sharply, " you don't take my proposal in a very friendly way. I imagine I am doing you a good turn too. It is not every man would do so in my position ; for, after all, she treated me very badly. However, we needn't go into that. I will write her a letter if you like—now, indeed, if you like ; and won't you stop a day or two here before going back to Kingston ? "

Mr. Trelyon intimated that he would like to have the letter at once, and that he would consider the invitation afterwards. Roscorla, with a good-humoured shrug, sate down and wrote it, and then handed it to Trelyon, open. As he did so, he noticed that the young man was coolly abstracting the cartridge from a small breech-loading pistol he held in his hand. He put the cartridge in his waistcoat-pocket and the pistol in his coat-pocket.

"Did you think we were savages out here, that you came armed?" said Roscorla, rather pale, but smiling.

" I didn't know," said Trelyon.

One morning there was a marriage in Eglosilyan, up there at the small church on the bleak downs, overlooking the wide sea. The spring-time had come round again; there was a May-like mildness in the air; the skies overhead were as blue as the great plain of the sea; and all the beautiful green world was throbbing with the upspringing life of the flowers. It was just like any other wedding, but for one little incident. When the bride came out into the bewildering glare of the sun, she vaguely knew that the path through the churchyard was lined on both sides with children. Now she was rather well known to the children about, and they had come in a great number; and when she passed down between them, it appeared that the little folks had brought vast heaps of primroses and violets in their aprons and in tiny baskets, and they strewed her path with these flowers of the new spring. Well, she burst into tears at this; and hastily leaving her husband's arm for a moment, she caught up one of the least of the children—a small, golden-haired girl of four—and kissed her. Then she turned to her husband again, and was glad that he led her down to the gate, for her eyes were so blinded with tears that she could not see her way.

Nor did anything very remarkable occur at the wedding-breakfast. But there was a garrulous old lady there, with bright, pink cheeks and silvery hair; and she did not cease to prattle to the clergyman who had officiated in the church, and who was seated next her.

"Indeed, Mr. Trewhella," she said, confidentially, "I always said this is what would come of it. Never any one of those Trelyons set his heart on a girl but he got her; and what was the use of friends or relatives fighting against it? Nay, I don't think there's any cause of complaint —not I! She's a modest, nice, ladylike girl—she is indeed—although she isn't so handsome as her sister. Dear, dear me, look at that girl now! Won't she be a prize for some man! I declare I haven't seen so handsome a girl for many a day. And as I tell you, Mr. Trewhella, it's no use trying to prevent it; if one of the Trelyons falls in love with a girl, the girl's done for—she may as well give in——"

"If I may say so," observed the old clergyman, with a sly gallantry, "you do not give the gentlemen of your family credit for the most remarkable feature of their marriage connections. They seem to have always had a very good idea of making an excellent choice."

The old lady was vastly pleased.

"Ah, well," she said, with a shrewd smile, "there were two or three who thought George Trelyon—that was this young man's grandfather, you know—lucky enough, if one might judge by the noise they made. Dear, dear, what a to-do there was when we ran away! Why, don't you know, Mr. Trewhella, that I ran away from a ball with him—and drove to Gretna Green with my ball-dress on, as I'm a living woman! Such a ride it was!—why, when we got up to Carlisle——"

But that story has been told before.

LONDON: PRINTED BY WILLIAM CLOWES AND SONS, STAMFORD STREET
AND CHARING CROSS.